I NEVER LIKED YOU ANYWAY

This novella re-imagines the Afterlife in a way you haven't seen before. It is a fun and poignant ride towards discovering one's purpose and identity. But ultimately, a love letter to life itself.

Eugenia Triantafyllou

An irreverent, modern take on the myth of Eurydice and Orpheus, this novella will have you laughing one moment and your heart breaking the next. Jordan Kurella has crafted a story full of music, wit, and love, an ode to the myths we embody and the ones we tell ourselves. With elements of straight and queer romance, and loads of rock'n'roll vibes, this book lands somewhere between Bohemian Rhapsody and Circe, and it's an absolute delight.

S.B. Divya

Copyright © Jordan Kurella

Published by Lethe Press | lethepressbooks.com

ISBN: 978-1-59021-739-9

This work is fiction, and any resemblance to any real person, dead or otherwise, is incidental.

Typesetting: Ryan Vance

I NEVER LIKED YOU ANYWAY

OR:
THE TALE OF
EURYDICE & ORPHEUS
AS TOLD BY ONE GOD
AND ONE MUSICIAN

Jordan Kurella

LETHE PRESS

THE AFTERLIFE:
PRESENT DAY

At three o'clock, standard Death Time, Eurydice must attend mandatory Threads of Fate sewing lessons. Eurydice hates them. Sewing fate should be interesting, but she is awful at it. At first, Eurydice must measure out the appropriate amount of time weighted by deeds. This is tricky, Eurydice has questions about deeds, and which deeds are good deeds and which deeds are bad deeds (and which deeds are good and bad only by perspective).

Eurydice asks a lot of questions.

It should come as no surprise that Eurydice is the sort to ask questions, the sort that get her in trouble. After all, it is how she got into the Afterlife. Eurydice is a terribly curious woman who went through life making bad decisions because, truly, one only lives once, and projecting oneself into the first available opportunity is a decision, after all. Sometimes, Eurydice asks so many questions that the Threads of Fate Instructor must call a short break due to a feigned headache. They require a cup of coffee. In these periods, Eurydice has time to speak to her best friend, Penelope. The conversations in these breaks sometimes go like this.

"Hey, friend," Penelope says. She is smiling yet concerned.

Penelope is often smiling yet concerned.

"Hey," Eurydice says back.

"What've you got going on after this?"

"I've got Creating Baking Disasters at five," Eurydice says.

"Of course, yes, Controlled Baking Chaos," Penelope says, and she nods the nod of one who knows something Eurydice doesn't. She has the posture of one who knows something Eurydice doesn't. Her weaver's fingers are curled under her angled chin, brown skin still keeping its tan complexion (even as in death), her black hair remains thick and today is drawn half back from her face.

But even without the posture, Penelope always knows something Eurydice doesn't; this is on account of being Penelope, and on account of how she pays attention and Eurydice does not. Eurydice was habitually terrible at paying attention.

Then, Penelope says, "I didn't pick that particular elective."

Eurydice says, "Which one?"

"The baking one," Penelope smiles. "I chose the other one."

"Other one?" Eurydice asks, parroting Penelope back at Penelope.

"Yes," Penelope says. "I chose Hauntings."

The word has weight. So much weight, in fact, that Eurydice makes the motion to take a breath, except even that pleasure has been stolen from her: the sort of people who take classes called Hauntings and Controlled Baking Disasters, are of course, learning to be better ghosts.

"Oooh," Eurydice says.

Exactly like a ghost. Very good, Eurydice.

At five o'clock, during Controlled Baking Disasters, Eurydice once again could not make her particular baker destroy their concoction. As usual, her baker's project came out perfect. Perfecter than perfect. As her instructor said every time, "Eurydice, you are simply not the sort to be in this class."

This is not news to Eurydice. Eurydice had always been not the sort to be anywhere. She was not the sort to be with Orpheus, Aristaeus proved that. She was not the sort to protect Andi; instead, Andi had to protect her. Eurydice doesn't know what sort of woman, or ghost, or person she is anymore.

In life and in death, she remains far too good to cause chaos and far too much of a disaster to make any sense of being good. This is why, at six o'clock, Eurydice drops Controlled Baking Disasters and is transferred to Hauntings. Partly because of Penelope, but partly because there's a particular person whose life she wants to make a particular hell.

I think we both know who.

His name starts with "Or" and ends with "Pheus."

EURYDICE:
MEMORIES

Never agree to marry a musician. I wish I could say that was my first mistake, or anyone else's, actually. But no, a person makes tons of mistakes in their life, tons. But the one, the big one, the one that led me to the end, was falling for Orpheus.

Oh sure, we initially liked each other. And then I guess we were in love. He wrote a whole suite for me, said he was inspired by me, said he needed me. It was the kind of codependency that was hot at the time when I was twenty and alive and breathing and lonely. All his swagger and attention, all for me. People turned their heads to see us walk by, and I drank it up. We were a thing on campus.

But I'm getting ahead of myself.

Never agree to marry a musician, but first, never fall in love with one.

Oh, but it was easy to fall for Orpheus: the tight jeans, the long wavy black hair, the swagger.

Oh, the swagger. Not to mention the songs and the smirks and the straight-up fucking passion he had for everything. He was a passionate student and musician. We'd yell at the television together, and we both loved that about one another. We talked about books and sunsets and all sorts of things.

Of course, all this happened in college, where this sort of pretentious romance is typical. I also died in college, which is atypical. It was a brief romance, an overture worthy of the Russian Romantics. Or maybe, if I'm complimenting myself: a concerto by Liszt.

They wrote stories about us, but they left out one crucial part: I was a musician, too. I wasn't bad, either. I wasn't gifted like Orpheus. I didn't have an innate ability for music like him. Unlike him, I had to work for years to get my aptitude. Orpheus just had Apollo on speed dial or something.

But again, ahead of myself.

I'll start at the beginning.

Like I said, Orpheus and I met and fell in love in college. The college was an institution known for its music department, with two cathedrals for singing and godsdamn organs all over the place. A dozen choirs and about three hundred acapella groups going around like ducks all quacking in unison over some song or another. Those of us with larger instruments (like me with my piano), practiced either in practice rooms or—when we were lucky—on an empty stage for better acoustics.

Everyone on campus thought they would be discovered as Katy Scary, Katy Perry's goth younger sister or something. But I think Orpheus only had the ego actually to do it, 'cause he was doing it from his private studio room, the one he commandeered by changing the lock. The one I happened that happened to be right next door to the room with the best damn piano on campus. My favorite piano, the one that sounded like it had an actual soul.

Or the one I loved only because Orpheus was right next door, and I had a mini-crush on him for the year and a half before I met him. Either/Or.

Everyone noticed Orpheus. It was hard not to: he looked like a cross between a young Robert Smith and a young Siouxsie Sioux, with the smiles to match. The day he walked into orientation, there was a collective gasp like everyone was gonna sing Ave Maria or something, but nobody did. It was just Orpheus. Just him. Nobody noticed me, though, I was just Eurydice—the girl so invisible that she shuffled her feet on the carpet, shocking herself by opening doors. (It was a habit. Particularly in February.)

Then, halfway through my sophomore year, I played piano, going through an Elton John/ Billy Joel phase while Orpheus was composing yet another suite of songs that made my heart want to escape my chest to scream at me to do something, anything with my gods-damned life. Orpheus's music shook the walls and my soul and made my teeth itch with want to be something, do something, fuck something.

I couldn't stand the three feet of distance anymore.

So, I shut the piano, grabbed my backpack, and left my practice room with my brain needling at me with what I know now, in hindsight, was practicality telling me: "You're making a terrible decision, Eurydice." And I was. I was making one of the worst decisions of my life. The first of many worst decisions in very quick succession.

What's life without really bad decisions, though? So, of course, I stepped the three feet of distance to Orpheus's door, where I could feel the vibrations of his dissonance in my heart, in my bones, in my pants. It was lust that made me turn the doorknob to his practice room.

It was bad luck that he'd left the door unlocked.

This was how I first found Orpheus: alone, crouched over, lower back exposed, programming the drum machine in all that cacophony. All his recording gear was set up, his two vintage King Snake guitars and battered Gibson bass and an ancient MOOG keyboard. I shut the door behind me, trying to be subtle, but the haze of cigarette smoke and sweat and ozone had been pierced by acrid carpeting and fluorescent light. It was too late. He noticed me. He turned a knob on the soundboard. The thrum of his sound loop stopped, leaving us to both to *Ummmm* in silence with the idle amps and hesitation of my heart.

He told me up to the day I died that he swore he thought I was some muse come to bless him. Funny that.

"Hello?" he said rather than asked.

Fuck, even his voice sounded like sex, or I was just that thirsty.

"Hey," I said.

"You like the music?" He asked. Then he grinned, then he winked.

"Uh, yeah," I said. "That's why I'm here."

"Cool." He stood and brushed the months of carpet dust from his knees. "So, can you lock the door?"

So, slightly confused and way overwhelmed, I locked the door. What the hell did I just step into? But I stepped into it anyway: the room, Orpheus's life, and a whole mess of bullshit.

But he smiled, and his smile was also like sex.

"That was part of a suite, right? A loop with added instruments?" I asked, glancing at anything that wasn't him. At the overfull ashtray and litter of ash around it. At the wires snaking around the floor like adders. Then, at his boots, scuffed and mistreated like his bass amp.

"Yeah," he said, brushing his hair away from his face. "A little thing I'm working on."

"Um," I said. "I hate to say it, but I think one of the guitars was in a slightly dropped tuning. Did you mean to do that?"

"It was?" He glanced at the two King Snakes. "Oh shit, that's not supposed to be that way. Thanks. Thanks for telling me." He went to one of the guitars and started tuning it, the telltale sound of adjusting strings drawing out the silence. "You're right, this one is way off. Thanks."

Then, he looked me over like he was studying me for errors. I'd seen the same look on my composition instructor's face: looking over my work as if he wanted to find something wrong, and then the look of *Eureka!* on his face when he found it.

I braced myself for the exclamation.

But there wasn't one. Orpheus just flipped a switch on the soundboard and hit a pedal and started playing. "You wanna hear in a second, now that I got everything where it needs to be?"

"Uh. Yes."

I couldn't say it fast enough.

Orpheus finished playing, flipped the switch on the soundboard, and started flipping more switches, playing with a recording program I recognized from an old girlfriend's computer. Except she used it to record spoken word. I stood back, tipping from heel to toe, watching him stumble over himself to impress me.

I was stumbling over myself to impress him. It was mutual bullshit.

He turned with a feigned lack of enthusiasm and offered me a set of headphones, careful that our fingers barely touched. His gaze lingered on mine just a moment when it did, like he was testing the tension, just figuring me out. Wondering if this was the beginning of something or the end of something.

We were musicians, playing with each other in concert. We both knew how this worked. This was not a refrain, this was the slow, quiet build of a Tchaikovsky piece. The strings were just getting started. I put the headphones on; that's when the whole ass orchestra joined in. I was hooked.

Orpheus's music was something like if you took Philip Glass and made him smash with Sonic Youth: the kind of thing that made you uncomfortable to admit you were into, but when it was on, the floodgates opened. Whatever the fuck he was doing, it rendered me inert and speechless: my body erupting into goosebumps. There's a word for that when you're stunned to silence by something so awesome but damned if I could remember it right then. Or anything right then. I was too busy being hooked, caught.

I was trying to catch every dissonant harmony, every wayward note. Every drowning drumbeat. The melodies howled like lonely cats; they were answered by a chorus of wolves. I couldn't believe my ears; this was genius. And there I was, next door, trying to be the next piano-pop sensation. Everything, my entire life, felt very silly and forfeit.

I could drown in how beautiful his music was.

When the song was done, Orpheus tapped the headphones, not my shoulder.

"Hey, you okay?"

"Yeah," I said. "Yeah, I'm super okay."

"Did you like it?" he asked with eyes wide and hopeful as whole notes.

"Damn, Orpheus," I said, handing back the headphones with shaking fingers. "That was really, really good."

Orpheus smirked in a way that made me want to hold him, kiss him. Definitely kiss him. I made every effort not to show my feelings, but they were written in every action I took. I had to say something else to prove that I didn't want to kiss him. So, of course, I failed.

"I'm not joking around," I said. "I mean, really, this is some really good stuff."

He stepped back from me, taking me in, spreading his arms, palms out like Hermes. He wasn't taking me in academically this time, this was a long look up and down, the way men look at women when they want something. And I hadn't dressed any way worth wanting: my magenta angled bob was too long, too greasy, and too faded. This was day three of no shower, and my t-shirt was a laundry day special, paired at least with my favorite jeans. The ones so soft and comfortable they may as well be sweatpants. It was my most comfortable, least flattering presentation.

I did not feel at all presentable.

He, of course, looked perfect. Orpheus always looked perfect. Black mess of hair falling precisely to his shoulders. His perfect angled chin with two days of stubble peeking out and making him look like a cross between Don't Care and Do Care. He was skinny, so skinny, and his faded concert t-shirt had once fit him better, and so had his jeans. I'd talk about his belt, but I don't want it to seem like I was staring too much.

"Eurydice, right?" he asked.

Not gonna talk about how I was super surprised he knew my name, but I was.

"Yeah," I said. "That's me."

As if it could be anyone else.

"You play piano. You gave a Chopin recital last semester."

"Yeah, I did."

"It was wonderful," he said, in a way that he meant it. Told by the way his shoulders fell, the way his body relaxed, the way his breath sighed on the word *wonderful.* "What are you working on now?"

"I'm sort of going through a piano pop phase right now."

"Why." A statement, not a question. "You're a talented classical pianist, why would you swap over to pop music. Why would you throw skill away like that?"

I shrugged. I didn't know. Honestly? I didn't think I was ruining it, but standing in front of Orpheus and listening to that masterpiece suite, I felt like a charlatan. Like pop music was the easy way out when it really wasn't. Maybe I was ruining my life, was the sudden thought. Maybe Orpheus was right. Orpheus was right about a lot of things; he had his own private studio, had the adoration of the professors and the students and the administration. What did I have? Burgeoning carpal tunnel and hardly enough cash to do laundry. I believed what he said. Maybe if I listened to Orpheus, we could make out, and maybe if I made out with Orpheus, all my problems would be over. Maybe if I told him what he wanted to hear, then, then.

So, this is what I told him:

"It's not something I'm planning on sticking with," I said. I lied.

"Don't." Orpheus shoved his hands in his pockets, looking at me earnestly now. Like a colleague. "Don't do it. Stick to classical piano. That's where your passion is; your talent is."

"That sounds smart."

Complimenting him was easy. Too easy. I fell into it the way a person could fall into dancing in 4/4 time. A step here, a step there, and voila, you're dancing. Orpheus at least pretended to listen to me, so I continued to compliment him: the seduction of being the center of attention was too much. A smile here, a nod there, and voila, I was thinking about sleeping with him.

"You wanna come listen to something else later? I'm working on the next movement tomorrow."

"Tomorrow?"

"Yeah." He started packing up, setting the Gibson on its stand. "You... do you drink?"

"I don't," I said, still lingering.

"Do you drink coffee?" Orpheus was standing closer to me, smirking that smirk that won me over so hard.

"I do."

"Wanna go out for coffee? Like, right now?" A new kind of grin from him, one I hadn't seen yet. One that lit up his eyes with a different kind of mischief.

I matched that grin right back at him and said, "Sure do."

THE AFTERLIFE:
PRESENT DAY

Eurydice has a best friend in the Afterlife: Penelope. Like all other souls, Eurydice can also eat things in the Afterlife. Currently, she is having baklava, and licking the honey off her fingers, the way that young people sometimes do. Penelope is sitting with her ghostly fingertips on a cup of just-right temperature cardamom tea and looking off at the grey-on-grey horizon.

That said, there is something to be said about both best friends and baklava. Having neither truly is a crime. The Afterlife should be pleasant after all, as it is simply a stop-gap before the eternal boredom of constant reincarnation until the soul eventually gets their proverbial fates in a row (and can move Beyond).

The Afterlife is pleasant, as it's designed to be (except for the classes, which are litmus tests). As if a soul can manage fate, ruin cakes, or haunt the unhauntable, a soul can move Beyond. If they cannot, they're doomed to reincarnation. And if a soul can do neither, well, that's Sisyphean Tragedy.

I guess.

As for Eurydice and Penelope, their friendship is borne of convenience, the way that many short, quick, doomed friendships are. It is a friendship of Might As Well Do This rather than the proverbial Ride or Die, as they are both already dead and are both aware of their situation's temporary nature. Yet in their ways they both need one another. They have so much in common, each of them with issues with men starting with O: Orpheus and Odysseus respectively.

Before Penelope died, she enjoyed some time alone with neither Telemachus nor a suitor. She tossed her late husband to the waves and wove him into her narrative like a man forgotten and lost to time, a legend from long ago rather than a man whom everyone remembers (and Penelope herself a woman, too, whom everyone remembers). But Penelope is here to make her own story for herself, she says to Eurydice.

Eurydice appreciates that. She wants to do the same. To learn from her friend.

In all friendships, there are ebbs and flows, quiet times, and times of hot drama and action. In Penelope's and Eurydice's brief tenure of friendship, there are rarely quiet moments. It is almost all hot drama and action, as this morning, before the sun could hint at a presence through this grey expanse of clouds, Eurydice woke up to prayers from Orpheus.

"At first," Eurydice says, "I thought they were weird dreams, you know?"

She is still licking the baklava from her fingers, as she would in life. Penelope does not mind. She once did the same, back in life when she was Eurydice's age. Except royal standing and being surrounded by the hungry eyes of men stopped her from such practice.

She thinks, watching Eurydice now, that she should pick it up again. So she does, licking a little from her fingers. It tastes off, not the way she remembers. Penelope continues anyway, just for the sensation before speaking.

"Dreams? Were they dirty dreams at least?" Penelope asks.

"I know, right? I wish. I think that's what the Threads of Fate Instructor was worried about when I told him about the dreams." Eurydice busies herself with a napkin before she continues: wiping both hands and mouth. "But apparently, no, which is kind of a relief. Anyway, apparently the dreams I am getting are some sort of prayer? Like Orpheus is fucking praying to me?"

"Odd," Penelope says, doing the same with her napkin because it looked like a good idea. "I'd like to have some dirty dreams myself, but honestly, I'd settle for some prayers. Too bad we killed off all the men who thought I was hot."

"Yeah. Well. You're still hot."

"Even like this?" Penelope pushes her hair over her shoulder. "Thank you. That said, it's nice to be thought of? Maybe? Even a small amount?"

Penelope sets down her tea as she says that, lacing her fingers in front of her. Brown eyes narrowed in concern, the way she used to watch her son trying to make amends with his father, so many years ago.

"Not *really*? In the dreams, he says he wants me back, that he'll do anything, *anything*, to get me back."

"But how does he expect to get down here?" Penelope brushes her long, ephemeral hair from her face. "We're in Hades's realm. Does Orpheus not understand that? He can't get here. Unless like." She pauses, blinks, and cleans the table as if to clean away the frightening thought. "No, I'm not even going to say it."

It's Eurydice's turn to lean forward. And she does with the kind of rapt energy of a woman in her twenties, the kind of way that she has both a secret to share and a need to scream something profane at the top of her voice.

Except she doesn't. Because she's in my realm, and she knows I can hear it just fine, no matter how she says it. Which is true.

"But, Penelope," she says. "What if he can?"

EURYDICE:
MEMORIES

Coffee, of course, was a euphemism for sex, and Orpheus and I met up for "Coffee" several times those first few weeks. Whether we were in the music building and I was back to Chopin and Liszt and all that--he'd come sticking his head in the door. "Coffee?" And me? I couldn't get my shit together fast enough.

Or we'd be out at another generic party, him drinking flat lite beer, me drinking flat diet soda, and he'd look at me across another dimly lit room, both of us standing on another wet and sticky carpet in an apartment that smelled overwhelmingly of skunk weed and men's feet. But I didn't care. I was waiting for him to say it (I'd been waiting hours for him to say it, my teeth basically glued to one another at this point). Thing is, we both knew it.

We both knew how much we wanted each other, and this was part of the game: the tease. It was foreplay. He would make the wait agonizing by drawing out the long glances over my body, which would make me shiver. And then he'd ignore me, making me shiver more in that anticipatory way. We both knew it was going to happen, the coffee. It was just there.

He'd wave to the up-and-coming Katy Scarys. We'd talk to them, dance with them. When he danced, he'd put his hands where he was gonna put his hands later, and I would have to watch myself on the dance floor so that I wouldn't show too much. Sure, I'd never be Katy Scary, not in a thousand years. But I could be Orpheus's girlfriend. Maybe. Eventually.

Right now, whatever this was? This coffee thing? It was fine.

Then, when the music swapped to something too popular that *anyone* could dance to, Orpheus would drag his hands across my hips to my hand to my lips. Pull me in for a kiss, and we were off. So fast that by the time we got to his dorm room, our clothes made the floor even faster. And then he was on me before I could process it. Skin on skin, lips on lips (which lips didn't matter, I was into it). And then everything was slick and loud, and he was talking dirty to me, and his hair smelled like pomade and cigarette smoke, and his mouth tasted like me, and, and, and.

I never came.

But he did.

It didn't matter at the time, not in the beginning. We were new to each other, and cis men (as I knew) had an easier time at orgasms than I ever did. Or at least that's what I told myself. For a cis man, my body was like trying to figure out how to play flute when they were used to guitar. There was a whole bunch of delicate fingering and where to put the lips and the intricacies of pressure in order to make the prettiest and best sounds.

It's a crap analogy, but I'm going with it.

My body to anyone else but a cis man was like playing *Twinkle Twinkle Little Star* on the violin. Everyone gets it, some better than others. Some really well enough to improvise a little and make those stars shine.

After every "coffee," Orpheus and I would lay naked, side by side, sharing a cigarette and talk about what we wanted out of our ideal musical future. He wanted to play Lincoln Center. I wanted to also play Lincoln Center. So, of course:

"What if we collaborated?" he asked, running his hand along my steady thigh.

"Collaborated?"

"Yeah, like, what if worked together on our music, like a team."

He was looking at me in that post-coital haze that he got where he'd say anything to draw me in further and further and further. My experience with cismen here was that usually they told me they loved me and that they wanted to marry me. Which usually sent me running away. But this was different. This actually did pull me in.

"A team, like a *team* team?"

"Yeah, you and me make music together."

"I'd like that," I said. "I'd really like that."

The next few days, he brought it up casually. Over lunch (broccoli and cheddar soup for me, chicken nuggets for him). Working together, collaborating. The idea fell off over the next few weeks after weeks. But we were seen together more. He even held my hand as we walked through campus, now the site of both of us: rockstar Orpheus and me, the invisible Eurydice, a couple.

How shocking.

"You'd be better use as kindling!" yelled someone, I assumed at us.

But it was an upright bassist yelling at the towering pines that dropped their needles all over the stone paths. Making their walks from building to building nigh unnavigable. Orpheus used to walk staring up at those trees, now he stared at our feet together, walking in tandem.

"Your shoes are cute," he said once. "All scuffed up and adorable. Like you."

I honestly didn't know how to take that.

He'd walk past storefronts downtown and not catch his reflection, but I couldn't help looking at the two of us, both of us warped and twisted like horrific versions of ourselves. We always looked like Clowns on World Goth Day.

It was nice, cause for the first time, people were noticing *me*. People started coming to my recitals because Orpheus was there. People started asking me how to perform as I did at my recitals: taking notes and tips on their phones, supposedly, but probably texting or playing some mobile game. Orpheus said he loved my recitals 'cause I made the performance aspect a huge part of it. He said that Tori Amos could pack her piano up, 'cause compared to her, I was gonna resurrect Rachmaninov with how I moved on that bench.

But we were always alone, Orpheus and me. He kept me to himself, I kept him to myself. I had a couple of close friends, people from my freshman hall or people in the orchestra that I'd muscled up the courage to talk to.

"You've been busy," they said. "Gone a lot."

"Yeah," I said, swirling latte around with my finger.

"You're seeing someone, aren't you? You always ditch us when you're seeing someone."

"Uh," I said. 'Cause I got caught.

The two women looked at each other. It didn't matter whether it was two women from my dorm, or two people, or a couple of others from orchestra, they all knew this about me.

"You'll be back," one of them said. "You always come back."

Orpheus, however, had different tactics.

One time, after coffee, he got up and put on his pants rather than laying there and making blithe promises he never meant to keep. Pulled his shirt over still sweaty skin.

"Where're you going?" I asked, our cigarette still in my hand.

"My friends wanna meet you," he said. "There's a campfire, c'mon."

"Your friends want to meet me," I said.

"Yeah," he said. "I've been telling them all about you, and they think you sound super cool. Cause I think you're super cool."

I smiled at him, stubbing the cigarette out in his overfull ashtray. "You think I'm super cool?"

"Yeah," he said, smiling at me with that same smirk that made me fall all over him three weeks ago. "I do. I like you a lot, Eurydice. I *like* you like you. You're my girlfriend."

"I'm your girlfriend?"

He'd never said it before.

"Course, but like not my exclusive girlfriend." He sighed, fixing his hair in the mirror. "I haven't been sleeping around on you cause we haven't been talking about this, but I'm poly, always have been. Is that okay? I'm not straight."

I smiled, also sighing with relief.

"I'm not straight either, and I've done the polyamory thing before. I can do it again, no big deal. As long as you're cool with it? Me not being straight?"

"As long as you're cool with me not being straight."

He turned and looked at me, a wounded man. Totally gutted, like he admitted to me something he'd been holding in for months. And it'd been almost two months that we'd been sleeping together. So, I guess he had been holding it in. Poor guy.

Not poor guy.

I slid out of his bed, still naked, and wound my arms around his waist, kissing him on his neck. "I like you a lot, Orpheus. We'll make this work."

"Okay." He placed his hands on mine, lacing our fingers together. "Just don't go jumping into another relationship right away, it'll make this one feel cheap."

"You got it."

He, in fact, did not get it because we arrived at the campfire, and there *they* were. Andromeda (aka Andi): the person who would teach me self-worth and self-acceptance and bring my whole life to a glorious confusion, and the person that I'd start pining when they said, "I think there's a hole in the bottom of your cup cause you have 'coffee' all over your pants, Eurydice."

I melt for that kind of honesty.

THE AFTERLIFE:
PRESENT DAY

At Haunting class, Eurydice is trying to learn the art of being invisible, one of the fine arts of ghosting on earth. This may sound simple to some: fade into the background, do your best not to be seen. But being invisible is different than not being seen. Eurydice once had mastered the art of not being seen, she had thought (incorrectly), but being invisible? That's being neither anyone's shadow nor even the making faintest mew of sound.

But what a Haunting must evoke is a *feeling*.

A feeling while being both silent and incorporeal.

This is not a concept Eurydice is familiar with. As a musician, she once evoked feelings with performance, with a strike of the keys, with a touch on a shoulder or a brush of her fingers on someone's neck. Now she must do it with only the faint idea of presence.

Difficult for Eurydice.

It brings up feelings of her own.

When Penelope and Eurydice leave class together (again, always together), Eurydice strides ahead. Too far ahead for Penelope, who walks quietly behind, waiting for Eurydice to exhaust her fury of being too wrong of a ghost to do hauntings. Too wrong of a spirit to read fate. Too kind of a poltergeist to inconvenience others. Penelope watches Eurydice as I watch these two friends with my godsight.

My elbows are propped on the kitchen table while I eat another hot dog (and don't tell Persephone, but I'm feeding the scraps to whichever of Cerberus's three heads are fastest today).

Eurydice is fun to watch, I must say. But not in the way that voyeurs watch people in the mortal realm. That is not what I do here in the Afterlife. Here, in the Afterlife, everyone must be judged. But also here, in the Afterlife, one picks particular souls of interest, and I have had my eye on Eurydice for some while.

Penelope has had her mind on her only for a few weeks, or months, or hours. Time doesn't matter here in the Afterlife, although the bells pretend it does (they're fake). So, Penelope cares in that empty, soulless way a ghost can care. Eurydice cares too much about everything. Which is something I noticed upon her arrival. My wife, too. It is what we hoped for, that this passion for everything, this swagger of hers, would transfer to death.

And it did.

Lucky for us—confusing for Eurydice.

While my wife's supply of frozen hot dogs grows evermore slim, even this soon in the autumn, I think about rationing them (but I cannot, and I know this). Cerberus does not think about rationing them, only about dog things. Three sets of dog things. As for the hot dogs, there will be an end to them, as there is an end to everything.

This happens every year.

But that is not important. What is *important* is the fact that Eurydice is horrible at all her classes, which means she is destined to the terrible roulette of reincarnation, and according to my files, this has been a pattern for her: over and over and over again. Which is exactly what I wanted.

I sigh with contentment. Cerberus sighs with frustration.

Penelope also sighs, but with worry. It is a gentle sigh in a not-so-gentle place. Everything Penelope does is an attempt at gentle: the way she said goodbye to her son was attempted gentle; she even achieved saying farewell to her late husband gently. To her position in Ithaca: semi-gently. Telling those suitors to kindly go away and leave her alone for very many years: not so gently.

Penelope is semi-gentle/semi-sweet. Even when she doesn't mean to be. We all have our faults.

"It can't be all bad, Eurydice. You're not pushing a rock up a hill."

"Yet." Eurydice kicks a stone into the moors. They are in the moors, beyond the restaurants and parks and anywhere pleasant. Eurydice's fury and anger brought her this far. "Not pushing a rock up a hill, yet. I'm failing, Penelope. At this rate, I'm not going Beyond. At this rate? I'm gonna end up back at that college as a cockroach under Orpheus's boots. Just to be crushed again and again and again."

Penelope looks at Eurydice as if she wants to hug her, but the gesture would be insubstantial. They both know that. They look at each other as if the hug is given and accepted and bow their heads.

"Give yourself some credit," Penelope says. "You're a rat, at least."

"Thanks."

"A big and powerful rat. You'll probably bite Orpheus a couple times first."

They grin at one another, turning to look at the grey-on-grey horizon as what passes for a sun here sets behind them. It is always grey in the Afterlife. What should be black is more like slate grey. Even the moors are dotted with grey heather and pussy willows. Grey like the proverbial rat? Perhaps. I always preferred brindled ones, myself.

As they look out at that horizon, in their long silence, they both know that Penelope is right. And so do I. "More hot dogs, boys?" I ask the dog. Dogs? No one's ever been clear on that.

Crouching down, I open the freezer and realize that, terror of terrors: we are out.

EURYDICE:
MEMORIES

And then there were two. Andi and Orpheus. Andi was the sort of person who wore their hair thick and long and black down their back and collected the frizziest cardigans from the thrift store. They were as tall as me with thick black wavy hair. They were Korean, except they'd say, "I'm Korean in that way that pisses people off 'cause I'm not Korean in the way they expect Korean people to be Korean." They'd then shrug and light a cigarette.

Andi was my favorite of Opheus's friends, so much my favorite that when we looked at each other, they'd usually say, "Wanna go get some air?" And I'd sigh cause with Orpheus and Andi in the room, there was really no more air left.

Orpheus's friends were the sort of pretentious pompostors who took up every second of oxygen to talk about how great they were and also every inch of space to lounge as if Brian Eno were composing Great Dane. Their legs and arms dangling everywhere in an incomprehensible way. It was frankly exhausting, Andi was the most grounded of the lot. They were also the only Econ major, which was a little out of my league. But so was Orpheus, so why not go for two?

Orpheus had picked up a boyfriend while I was admiring Andi. Aristaeus. Aristaeus with messy black hair, different enough from Orpheus's so that they didn't look like twins. While Orpheus looked like an 80's goth relic, Aristaeus cultivated a Jack White lookalike contest reject aesthetic. He had a snake tattoo running up his arm, where the fangs struck his and second and fourth fingers (leaving the middle one free). Aristaeus was also the type to check his watch to see if a polite-ish enough time had passed before he could interrupt. Again.

Everything about Aristaeus was *heavy.* His talking points were heavy, he wore heavy leather jackets; he stepped heavy, his presence was heavy. Just being around him made me tired. So ever since Aristaeus entered into the friend group (about a week after the campfire, about two days after Andi and I started hanging out), I started hanging around Andi more.

A lot more.

Orpheus noticed a little bit. He liked Aristaeus, I could tell by the way the two couldn't keep their hands off one another (the same way he couldn't keep his hands off of me). Except with Aristaeus, the affection was public. With me, it was private. Behind closed doors, in his practice room, in mine, when I had it reserved.

When Aristaeus and Orpheus were together, the room was electric with tension: all sorts. I needed to get the fuck out. So, Andi and I did. For walks along the leaf-littered paths, for coffee (actual coffee), or to sit by the creek that ran by the school and talk while Orpheus and his buddies sat and talked and Great Dane'd about inside.

One of these afternoons, about three weeks into pining after Andi, and three weeks after Orpheus pawing over Aristaeus, I had another conversation by that creek. With Andi, not Orpheus. Andi hand-rolled their own cigarettes in a crunchy, wanna-be-holistic sort of way, but really they said it gave them more to do with their hands.

They told me they were always fidgety. Hence the smoking, rolling their own cigarettes, and the super pilly cardigans. It offset the air of practicality that surrounded them. It gave them an edge that just made me want to be around them more.

"My parents'll kill me if I major in dance," they said one day while we were catching some air on the quad. Both sitting with our butts in the wet pine needles after another afternoon's rain.

"Immigrants, you know. So, when I got into college, I had to major in something useful. I figured major in economics, minor in dance. Then I'd get a job and a girlfriend at the clubs. You know, on the weekends with my super slick moves."

They turned and grinned at me. I mirrored that grin right back.

"See, my parents didn't mind the music thing by the time they got to me," I said, scooching some pine needles away with the toe of my boot. "Cause, I have two sisters."

Andi just nodded, moving some pine needles away with their foot. Chewing on their lips and exhaling slightly. There was something being left unsaid, but they weren't saying it.

"Anyway." I sighed, opening and closing my fists on my knees. "One's of my sisters is a pediatrician. *And* married. The other is a lawyer, and divorced."

"Sounds like you made the right choice, being a musician."

I nodded, looking at Andi, who was looking at me. Looking at me with longing, the three inches of space between us being too much. The crisp fall air being too cold. I wanted their warm arms around me. To feel their frizzy, pilly cardigan tickling the back of my neck. I wanted to give them something to do with their hands.

I wanted to say, "Can I kiss you?"

But I didn't, not yet.

What I said was, "Not everyone gets to be a musician."

And what they said was, "Only the best do."

Their smile was sad when they said it, pushing their hair away from their face, exposing their rounded jawline that I wanted so much to reach out and touch in that moment. To tuck their hair behind their ear for them. But instead I watched them roll another cigarette, so I lit one of my own.

Instead, I thought about them.

Andi's voice was husky, tinged with gravel. If they were a singer, they'd be Tom Waits. If I was a singer, I'd be kicked out of the piano bar. Andi's fingers were long and beautiful but stress-eaten: cuticles shredded, nails bitten. Their lips were as well. Always red and raw, their honey lip balm never too far away. But unlike me, Andi gave every pretense of being in control. Whereas me: I was out of control. In my fashion sense, behavior, and everything I said.

Andi was a haunted house.

I was just a wreck.

THE AFTERLIFE:
PRESENT DAY

At Threads of Fate classes, Eurydice is trying to concentrate on the present. Not the past deeds of the individual whose thread she holds in her hand, not the very fact that she, Eurydice, will choose the final act of their death (just as someone chose hers, a death she still considers to be wholly unfair). She is trying, as the Instructor has told her over and over again, to look at the thread the way she would look at any sewing thread.

But Eurydice was always shit at sewing.

It was Penelope who was the weaver.

Penelope is a master at Threads of Fate classes. The Instructor often comes by her work, praising her and using her expertise as an example. Penelope's constant obfuscation of deeds done and heroism into the final days of one's life is part of her own history (as is famous at this point). She still believes that Odysseus got the death he deserved: not a hero's death, not a king's death, but a death of a man who had done wrongs, who had wronged others, and must--indeed--pay for that.

Unlike Eurydice, Penelope has zero chill when it comes to cutting threads.

Eurydice, as always, too much. She brings her own personal baggage to total strangers' lives, as she always did. "Those poor people are stranded by the side of the road," she'd say on a family road trip. "What if they need help? What if they're in trouble?" And her sisters would play handheld video games while her father continued to drive, leaving Eurydice to wring her hands, her own device forgotten in her lap.

Perhaps she would've been better served as a social worker than a musician, but the Fates didn't see it that way. And frankly, neither do I now, at Persephone's behest. We are both thrilled to have her here.

The Instructor, however, is not. They float over to Eurydice once again. She is still on her first thread of the day, while Penelope is on her fourth, other members of the class on their third or at least second.

"What is it, Eurydice. What is it this time?" Their voice is echoey, echoing the insubstantial nature of the Instructor themselves. They have no feet and no face. They exist simply as a robe and a voice. Exuding shadow and authority.

They currently hover over Eurydice's workstation as she holds the golden thread, delicate as water in her hands. She looks up at them, "I just. Maybe what if this one—"

The Instructor halts her once again.

"Do not consider what could have been, only consider what was. Do not look so far in the past, only at the last years of the individual's life. A person's death is not the sum of their entire years, but only their final actions." They pause, bobbing up and down a few times before speaking. "Eurydice."

"What? Instructor?"

"Are you putting too much personal investment in this person's life again?"

There is no need for an answer. Eurydice looks down at her hands, at the shimmering gold that runs back and forth like a living thing. She chews on her lip. That is all the Instructor needs to know.

"This person is not you, will never be you."

Then they leave, echoing chill and shadow in their wake.

Eurydice tries to follow their instructions while idly watching them visit Penelope again for small talk. She is not jealous, she tells herself. She isn't (she is). But she is now convinced she is going nowhere but back to earth to relive her mistakes as a cockroach.

EURYDICE:

MEMORIES

Andi took me to see a horror musical playing the local playhouse. The musical was gory and so, so bad. The singing was overwrought, the lighting even more so. It was so dramatic and overdone that it gave me ideas: ideas like how to make Chopin really choppin', and how to actually make Liszt more lippy.

As for Andi, their breath caught every time a heroine got stabbed. They reached out for my hand when it happened. But we weren't there yet, we hadn't talked about it. But I wanted their hand on mine, so I let their fingers brush mine.

When they finally did, Andi looked at me and sighed.

We both chewed our lips so much that mine were red and raw by the time we exited. The November hit them harder than I'd bit them, stinging them with that kind of harshness that only November can provide. Andi's ash-stained (once caramel-colored) coat whipped around them as they tried to light a pre-rolled cigarette. I kept my hands in the pockets of my own faux-leather bomber, deciding not to navigate this.

"Can you block the wind for me?" they asked.

So I did. And when I did, I noticed that Andi's hair smelled like drug store conditioner and ashtrays. A combination that made me weak. Orpheus's smelled the same. I had to layer my own down with argan oil and mousse, so it smelled rancid by the end of the day. So attractive, I'm sure, but not applicable now.

After ten flicks of the lighter and no actual flame, Andi put the cigarette behind their ear and the lighter back in their pocket. "Let's go find some actual shelter so we can both have a smoke," they said. "You're awesome but too damn skinny to be a windbreak."

I laughed. They laughed, and we went around the wall of the theatre to the Employee Parking and the dumpsters, somehow, always kept right next to each other (because that's what businesses think of their employees, let's be real).

We lit our cigarettes and passed small talk about the musical. Who was hottest on a scale of 1-10, who we shipped with whom 'cause the musical didn't really allow for that, which outfits we liked best and which we would actually wear IRL. The usual.

Once my cigarette was out and Andi was crushing theirs under their foot, they looked at me and squared their shoulders. "Okay, serious question time."

"Alright," I said. "I'm ready."

"Can I kiss you?" they asked, nearly falling over the words. "I really want to kiss you."

I nodded. Before I could open my mouth to say "Yes, please," Andi's smoky gloves were on my cheeks and their lips were on mine and holy shit, we were kissing. My own fingers went to their hair, and my own lips responded back: bit as they were, raw as they were.

Andi made them even more raw.

We fumbled for one another. Our feet slipped on wet leaves and greasy popcorn butter until (in our feverish state) we fell against the dumpster, kissing even harder. Andi tasted like honey lip balm and cigarettes. Their split cuticles tangled in my dry, overdyed hair. But I didn't care. Our breath made clouds around us as our hands searched for bodies underneath coats, as our thirstiness thundered against single pane dumpster steel.

Like trash, Andi's kisses were sweet and hung around for a long time.

Even more like trash, our entire relationship was a dumpster fire: hot, burning, emergency after emergency. We were total weirdos, just trying to have a good time. Just trying to fall in love in a world that sure would allow it, but. Well, no spoilers.

Andi and I held each other so long after that kiss, our bodies cooling and our breath kissing each other's cheeks. It was a moment before we noticed the woman staring at us. The woman holding not only a dog on a leash but also a hefty bag of dog shit. Both woman and dog were wide-eyed and open-mouthed, and both Andi and I skittered and slid out of the way to let this woman do her trash business rather than deal with the two of us.

Yet, she said, even with both of us out of the way. "I... I need to throw this away."

"By all means," Andi said, looking anywhere but at her. "Don't mind us, we're also pieces of shit."

The woman stared for a couple of moments longer, and then, dog-doo still in hand, she turned and snapped the dog leash. Dog turned happily and followed, thrilled just to be included. Relatable, actually.

That night, Orpheus was hunched over his keyboard and overflowing ashtray working on a paper that was due in three weeks. He'd learned this tactic from me: space out writing time, work less, stress less. When he heard me come in, he threw his sinewy, muscled arm over the back of his chair, half turning to greet me.

"So," he said, his voice encapsulated in a raised eyebrow. "How was the play?"

"It was," I said. I began. And then stopped.

"That good, huh?"

And then he smiled. That smile that was like sex. That smile that I remembered from when I first met him in that room where he was playing that music; the music that sent me to outer planes made my whole body electric and wanting. Made me think only of him. He knew it had this power over me 'cause he stood and swept over to me, also sweeping my messy hair from my face.

"You like them?" he asked. He asked as he took my hands, still cold 'cause the heat in my car went out years ago.

"I, yeah."

"I like you too, Eurydice," he said, brushing my hair from my face. "I like you a lot. But you know that."

My whole body fluttered before he kissed me. I kissed him back, gripping his hands so hard that my short-ass nails bit into the palms of his hands. He threw my hands over my head and pushed me against the door, still kissing me, where I let my hands fall over his shoulders.

When we came up for air, I said. "I like you too, Orpheus. A lot a lot."

"Shh," he said. "Keep kissing."

"Oh gosh, yes."

And we did. One of his hands cupped my chin, the other pressed against the door for balance. My arms wrapped around his neck, teeth pulling at his lower lip as he pressed his knee between my legs. And I made the noise he liked. I made the noise 'cause I could do this with both: Andi and Orpheus.

My body could have both, my heart could have both, my lips could have both. But could I juggle the two of them? With college and music lessons and my thesis and...

I'd figure that out later.

I'd have to.

The next day, in piano lessons, my fingers were awkward. Like string cheese on the keys. My instructor sat next to me.

"Again," he said. His voice clipped and gaining in annoyance every time I started over on warm-up scales. And I stumbled over them every time, like I was falling down the stairs.

After ten minutes of this, my instructor turned to me, peering over the edge of his reading glasses (which I honestly think he wore all the time to look smarter). He folded his bronze-brown hands on his skinny-ass knees and took a deep, shaking breath.

"All right, Eurydice, out with it. What has got you so butterfingers today? Is it a boy? A girl? Are you hungover? On drugs? What is it?"

"Both," I said.

He looked stern, then concerned, then curious. Then everything at once.

"I mean, uh." I had to fix this. "I have a boyfriend and a partner."

Now I, too, folded my uncooperative fingers on my own knees and took a breath. I had no glasses to peer over, so I just lifted my chin and peered down my nose. That last part was hard 'cause I was about six inches shorter than my instructor in my platformiest boots. Problem was, I could now not escape his Drakkar Noir cologne.

"I'm not hungover. I don't do drugs. I don't even drink." There, now I sounded pretty square, except for the sex bit. I sounded like a dry, teetotaling nymphomaniac.

My instructor did the thing that all adults do when they disapprove of someone, even though I was pretty sure he was only three or four years older than me. He pushed his glasses up his nose and cleared his throat.

"Well," he said, packing up the sheet music. Now I knew I'd fucked up. "If you're going to prioritize your *relations* over your *education* perhaps you need to think whether college is the right place for you, Eurydice."

Not what I wanted to hear. Especially from my instructor, who was the worst at the best of times, but the absolute worst at the worst of times. But he was the music department's best piano instructor, and he'd been teaching me for nearly two years.

"I'm... I'm not."

"You *are*," he said, standing and sweeping his hand through his thick black expensive haircut before turning away. His pant legs swish swish swishing against one another on his way to the door. Cheap fabric. His clothing gave the appearance of a frugal guy but I could tell by how nice his hair and skin looked all the time that he was anything but. "You are. And I will not teach you if you come to another lesson behaving like this again."

The door opened and shut on its well-oiled hinges and with its muted click. I sat in the soundproofed room listening to my internal screaming. Well, I'd have to figure my stuff out.

Eventually.

THE AFTERLIFE:
PRESENT DAY

We are often asked, "How does your marriage work so well, Hades? You and Persephone could not be more different." But that is gods looking from the outside. They do not see how alike we are, truly. We both enjoy the comforts of one another's presence and pine for one another when we are away.

Arranged marriages are an ancient custom, and yes, Persephone's and my marriage was at first arranged. At first, she made spring when she returned home happy from the doldrums of the Afterlife (renamed from the Underworld sometime in the 1970s as calling it the Underworld was deemed 'too depressing' by the Olympian Council). Now she does it as seasons are *a thing* one *expects.*

At one time, someone quoted the saying, "Absence makes the heart grow fonder." But Persephone then would answer, "It's truly just the hot dogs. He simply waits for me to bring home hot dogs." Which are an amazing American invention, and I must know where they came from so that I can make them here.

The truth is that absence does not make the heart grow fonder. I see this in Eurydice's face, in Persephone's face. The truth is, in so many people, absence is a balm, a healing salve. It makes the heart repair itself and grow stronger. Absence makes the heart *grow stronger*.

However, Orpheus still does not see it that way.

Orpheus is a patron of the ancient sayings.

"He just will not leave me alone," Eurydice says outside the Threads of Fate classroom at nearly three o'clock, Standard Death Time. "He wants me to give him some sign that I'm okay."

Penelope's eyes go wide, half in shock and half in what the hells. "He knows you're dead? How can a person ask if another person is okay if they're dead? And been dead for months? What is Orpheus's definition of okay?"

"No clue?" Eurydice sighs a ghost sigh. An insubstantial thing that only moves the shoulders as a gesture rather than does anything else. "And months? Maybe years? Maybe, I don't even fucking know how I'm supposed to give him a sign."

"Can I ask how you died again?"

"I died embarrassed." Eurydice looks at the nigh-silent hustle and bustle of spirits through the grey hallway. "Don't really want to go into it right now. My last words were awful. What were yours?"

"Probably like, 'Ouch, it hurts!' or 'Help me!' or something." Penelope also turns to watch the corral of spirits. "You know what I think? I think people who have really good last words have editors for relatives."

There's a longer pause. Penelope is likely right, from my own understanding.

"Anyway, you're asking for your Fate Thread, right? Like we talked about?"

"Oh yeah. That was a good idea," Eurydice says with a firm nod.

"Me too."

"Cause, like you said, if it's my life that's holding me back, might as well look at my life to see... what's holding me back? It makes less sense now that I say it out loud."

Eurydice shuffles her feet on the hallway tile. Penelope lifts her chin to the silent throng of souls filling the hallway. The bell strikes three o'clock, then the two women open the door.

"It makes sense," Penelope says quietly as they approach the Threads of Fate Instructor, who is hovering by their desk, waiting for the two.

"You two speak loud enough to wake the dead," the Instructor says, floating in their own insubstantial way, but speaking with their very substantial voice.

"So," Eurydice says. "Can I have my thread or not?"

The Instructor pauses, looming over Eurydice in all their ability to loom. It is what Instructors do best, loom. And then lurk. Speaking is third on their list of things they are best at.

"Yes," the Instructor says finally. "Yes, Eurydice. You may have exactly that."

Eurydice smiles, giving a thumbs up to Penelope.

The Threads of Fate Instructor turns away for a moment and then says, "Whether you're ready for it or not."

EURYDICE:
MEMORIES

Love is a distraction. Holy fuck is it a distraction. And young love more so. Orpheus with his perfect hair and his muscled arms and the way he'd trail his finger down my arm and say, "Just fifteen minutes. Fifteen minutes." Fifteen minutes of sweating and groaning and messy passion. Then? I'd rush back to my piano

After my instructor's warning, I had to be careful.

And then. Then there was Andi. Andi was dissonance to everything I'd known or been brought up to believe. They were intoxicating in my interest of them. They did everything backwards: they brushed their teeth before coffee, ate dessert before meals, and the biggest bit? They knew their way around fifteen minutes way better than Orpheus did. Or any cisman I'd ever been with.

However, I was in college to be a pianist. Not a wife, not a sidekick or a lover. I had to cut down on the quick fifteen minutes if I wanted to be a musician, cause I was here to provide fifteen minutes of joy or extasy to anyone listening or watching. Sometimes not even fifteen. Sometimes ten, seven. I had to be quick about it, and know my way around the keys better than, well, my instructor was right.

My whole body was part of my act, much like it was with Andi, with Orpheus. But I needed that energy for the piano, not for privacy. That's what I was here for. That's what I really wanted, to be a success, not to be suspended.

One-hundred-fucking percent.

But yet still the relationships persisted. Both with Orpheus and Andi. The longer and longer the relationships went on, the more and more I was torn between the two, my heart and time ripped and shredded like something from Stravinsky: passionate and messy and misunderstood. Andi treated me like an equal part of their entire life, asked me what I wanted out of life, out of the mini-fridge, in my coffee. Orpheus, however, treated me like a precious found object—started introducing me to people rather than keeping me mostly to himself in private.

"Have you met my girlfriend, Eurydice?" he'd say as I choked on my Diet Coke at yet another introduction to another batch of strangers.

And every time eager nods would pass over my body like it was some kind of store mannequin. Checking me out to see how I'd fare on the open market. Anatomical algebra.

Late at night, my phone would light up with one or two texts that said: "Hey," they said. "Hey come over. Hey I miss you." It was Andi, every single time. And every single time I'd throw on a jacket and my boots and be over at their room in less than six minutes.

"Closer" took less time to play than it took me to get to their room.

After two weeks, I was exhausted of tripling down. Tripling down on Andi, Orpheus, and music. Schoolwork got wedged in between like quick rests, gasps of breath taken by an unpracticed soprano. When I wasn't in my dorm room hammering out a paper or an assignment, I was haunting the hallways of the music building, signing up for my favorite practice room in the early morning, in the quiet after lunch. All so I could attack the keys with a passion I should've been reserving for sex. But now I had only for Schubert, for Rimsky-Korsakov, for Dvořák.

At the three-month mark, I was ignoring Orpheus and Andi. Romance has a minor key, just like music. And it, too, has its consequences.

Hindsight is a bitch, though. And this isn't about me whining about how I fucked up. This isn't about what I should have done and how I should have noticed what the fuck was up: this is about what I did and why no one, ever, ever,

ever should do that. Ever again.

We all make mistakes, though, and I made some big ones. One of mine was giving up on Elton John and Billy Joel and Tori Amos and all of that and going back to the greats of Chopin, Heller and Brahms, etc. Composers that I didn't want to play. However, my mistakes lead to some surprises. Cause after six months of practicing contemporary piano (and who the fuck knows how many years of classical piano), I'd learned a thing or two.

One: that I could compose my own shit.

Two: that some people don't like to be tossed aside for art.

THE AFTERLIFE:
PRESENT DAY

The weaver and the way. That's Penelope and Eurydice, basically. Sure, sure sure. Penelope calls some shots: like convincing Eurydice to talk to the Threads of Fate instructor. But truly it was Eurydice who never followed, she was the leader, always leaving Penelope to trail behind.

This is how the two women are walking now down a gloomy sidewalk. Perpetually gloomy, perpetual cloud clover, with a constant promise of sunshine. In the Afterlife, promise is paramount. A glimpse of what these souls can gain if they play their classes right.

But Penelope and Eurydice? They keep their eyes on the ground. Always.

Is this smart? Some of the Instructors have called them smart, intelligent even. But the outcome of the two women's actions, the result of their studies and their downcast eyes (plus their coffee dates and their conversations) has yet to be determined. As in the Afterlife, every action is weighed, scrutinized.

Much like the material world, these two women came from: this is also a surveillance state. Except here, I'm the one who's watching. Creepy? Maybe. But it's my job, leave me alone.

Eurydice is leading Penelope through a park. A park of rolling hills that in another, livelier place would have been covered in dogs playing with one another and sunbathers banking on that promise of sun. Perhaps there may have been rugby or football types. But here, where we are, there is only Eurydice and Penelope. The park is only grass, rolling hills of grass, and no one else.

As the social life in the Afterlife is almost as dead as the people in it. And the dogs? Well. Dogs always go Beyond.

"How many more days until my fate thread comes in?" Eurydice asks Penelope.

It's been three days. Three days of scoldings in Hauntings class and soft looks from the Threads of Fate Instructor and three days of even more prayers from Orpheus.

"No idea," Penelope says. "What do they say about patience?"

Penelope could hold a master class on waiting and patience.

"It's a virtue," Eurydice said. "But what's the point of being virtuous when I'm already dead? Right? I mean, everything's judged by now. I gotta pass these classes, and that's what decides." She sighs. "What's the point of waiting? What are *you* waiting for?"

By *you* she means *me*. And I hear it, of course. Her voice a wail on the wind, a siren's call, a hearkening back to so many things a person may find sad or beckoning. Waiting itself is sad and beckoning. It sits like a pit in one's stomach and weighs one down after a time. And for Eurydice it was doing just that.

"I keep waiting for Orpheus to shut up with his damn prayers," she says. "But he doesn't. He doesn't. He keeps contacting me, asking for some sign, some witness of me. What the hell is he doing back in mortal lands? I don't care, but I do. Then I keep waiting to get better at Hauntings or Threads of Fate. I keep doing what the instructors say. And. And I don't get better."

She turns to Penelope. Her best friend. The woman who does so well in all her classes. The woman who seems to have all the answers, all the time. Eurydice's eyes are full of all the questions she wants to ask. Questions like: Why did Orpheus date that asshole Aristaeus in the first place? Questions like: Where do you go if you can't pass any classes? Questions like: I don't know what I'm going to do, Penelope, when you go beyond.

Okay that's not a question. But Aristaeus is an asshole if I may interject. The sort of individual who didn't change from where he was when he knew Eurydice from where he is now after Eurydice died. He's even thriving; he's that sort of guy. While Orpheus may have been a victim of circumstance (his words in his own prayers), Aristaeus was the man who changed him, and Orpheus went along willingly.

So, are they both assholes? Both Orpheus and Aristaeus?

Well, they're not here. Yet.

But Eurydice isn't asking about Orpheus or Aristaeus (although she probably should). Because much of the time, souls don't ask the questions they should, only the questions they think they should. Eurydice does that here.

"Should I ask the instructor how much longer it's going to take?"

"Maybe?" Penelope says more than asks. "I don't know. I really don't."

Penelope says more than asks a lot of things to Eurydice. While a best friend, Penelope also doesn't want to always tell Eurydice what to do because Eurydice needs that. Because Penelope understands that nobody ever asks to marry a terrible man. One that would throw her away who knows what, just so that he could have his glory at the cost of one beautiful almost-wife. As the best friend, Penelope stands as Eurydice does, with the wind whipping her ghost tunic about her brown ankles, not minding the wisps of hair that fall in front of her face like she doesn't seem to mind anything. (Which is a side effect of once minding too much.)

Eurydice, like Penelope, has problems with boundaries.

"Okay," Eurydice says. "Okay, okay. Neither do I."

Her magenta dye job still imperfect in her ghost form. She tucks her hair behind her ear and adjusts the shoulder of her ghost tunic. She rolls up her sleeves and takes an unnecessary ghost breath before steeling her gaze forward at the horizon. A horizon covered in fog. (It is also always foggy in the Afterlife. What's the point if you know what lies ahead?)

And then, Eurydice set off, only in the way a soul can. With heavy intent and heart, but without a sound in the place but her own humming and Penelope's sigh as she follows behind her best friend in the afterlife.

EURYDICE:

MEMORIES

There are eighty-eight keys on a piano. Split into black and white, but not evenly. I used to tell Orpheus that I wished life was so simple, that people were cut the same way, so easily defined by their light and dark sides. I wished I could see them for what they truly were: in their bright and moody moments.

But, unfortunately, no one is like that.

Except Orpheus always replied: "Except you, Eurydice. You're exactly like that."

I was I then. I took it as a compliment, being so transparent (or opaque, whichever); I thought he was saying I was *real* and *genuine.* I valued that too much then, this need of mine to be an authentic—elf--to present this integrity (my integrity) to the world.

Hanging out with Orpheus and Aristaeus in their practice room ('s it'd become their practice room at this point since Aristaeus was just as talented as Orpheus when it came to music and the two of them wailed together in a Lisa Gerard-like keening that set my heart on fire), they talked about integrity a lot. The integrity of music and of people and h'w it's really only an *idea* of a thing.

I disagreed at the time, but I said I agreed 'cause I was in love. I think?

"Integrity's a clay," Aristaeus said. "You can make it a brand if you really want to. It's not a real thing. It's more like a skin people put on themselves. Kind of like kindness."

Orpheus nodded while he tuned his King Snake guitar.

"What do you mean, kindness is a skin?" I asked.

"No one is truly kind," Aristaeus said. "It's all fake. People are only kind cause they want something. Everyone wants something from everyone else in this world, and the true masterminds are just super nice about it. Which is why I don't go after kind people." He flipped his hair out of the way. "They're the true sociopaths."

Orpheus nodded again. "That's the fucking truth right there."

I tensed up my shoulders and dug my nails into my knees, cause that was the most bullshit thing I'd ever heard and I wanted out of the practice room. But Orpheus'd locked the door behind me, and I was now stuck in here with these two weirdos.

People'd warned me that Aristaeus was bad news: jealous, kind of sketchy, and a little on the intense side. Now I saw it for real, and I saw how he'd just brought Orpheus along for a ride on his ideology train, and Orpheus bought season tickets for the world tour.

I didn't like it.

Not at all.

But between us, nothing changed at all. He still kept coming to all my recitals, which were still packed as ever due not only to his presence but also to his talking me up. He continued throwing black roses onto the stage at those recitals, and I continued to love it. He kept insisting on my attention and introducing me to his friends and now the music department administration. I felt like I *had* to stick with him now if my career was going to go places.

Orpheus and Eurydice were an item. We were a thing. If I broke it off now, no matter how uncomfortable I was with Aristaeus's puke philosophy then, I'd ruin everything. *Everything.* So I had to stay, I thought I was being calculating, stringing Orpheus along. Keeping him around for his connections and his friends and all of that.

I was wrong.

He was always talking to me about my music, about my compositions. Asking me questions about how I did this and how I knew this phrase needed to follow that rest. Why I knew that the key change needed to happen at this moment rather than three bars before. it was cool, I thought. How he saw me as a peer when I thought he was way beyond me. I remembered his talk about collaborating, although he tossed that out the window for Aristaeus's collaboration. We talked about music over text, over the phone. He even emailed me once to ask for an attachment of one of my compositions. I was so excited I sent the wrong one.

He called me his muse, and I swooned.

Because the more orchestrated, careful, calculated attention he paid to me, the more attention I paid to him. I sat in his private studio room, the one filled with wires and the smell of ozone from too many plugs in too few outlets. I listened to more of Aristaeus's terrible oration and discussion (this time about how music isn't meant to be understood by the masses and the masses don't deserve music).

But when they got going: I sat rapt, my hands pressed tight between my knees, my eyes shut so hard it hurt. I sat and listened to every note, every rest, every refrain of his cacophonous delight of shaking hell.

And then, oh, did I quake to it.

While he waited outside my practice room, I sweated over my own eighty-eight keys of light and dark, not evenly distributed. I thought our relationship had become a neat partition of what

I hoped human life would be. While I played, humming to my own pianissimos, fingers raw by the end, only to find him on his phone when I exited, wild and eager for his reaction.

He told me I was brilliant every time. He always listened. He always had so much to say. We advised one another on this phrase and that crescendo. What would sound best in the next movement. Each of us was needed in our own growth. And Andi? Andi was our biggest fan.

One evening, as I was in my practice room and Andi's coat filled it with the smell of stale cigarette smoke and coconut conditioner, I attacked the piano with my latest composition. My entire body a riot with each note, then quieting, then attacking. It was the musical fury of Shostakovich with the performance art of Glenn Gould. I cited my musical inspirations as the 20th Century Russian composers, with the occasional chaos of Mussorgsky.

Andi lounged languidly on a spare piano bench, head resting on their hair, either texting their partner/my metamour Hector or listening to me while staring at the ceiling. I glanced over at them in between movements, and they were more engrossed in their phone than in me. After the second movement, I paused. Paused and threw my long leg over the bench and perched there, leaning toward them.

"What's up?" I asked. "What's wrong?"

"I liked your earlier stuff," they said, turning their perfect face toward me, putting the phone down. The one with the one dimple and the smile full of coffee and cigarette-stained teeth. "It sounded less like Orpheus and more like you."

My heart stuttered in my chest as I caught myself not breathing for more than a few rests. My fingers worried the scratched wooden bench, and I looked at them. At their well-tended cuticles and short, short nails. I forced myself to take long, slow, pretended yoga breaths.

"You okay?" Andi said.

They sat up and crossed the room, straddling the bench and placing their forehead on my forehead. I could smell their waxy honey lip balm. My arms reached for their shoulders and rested there for a while. A while so I could still breathe long and slow and harsh.

"No," I said finally. "No, I'm not okay."

"You want to sound like you," they said.

"Yeah."

"Then do it." Andi's hand reached for my cheek, fingertips playing in the wisps of hair at my ear. They exhaled, breath tickling my chin and neck. "Then sound like you. Be you, and not him. Always be you."

THE AFTERLIFE:
PRESENT DAY

There is not too much more time to wait for Eurydice to get her fate thread back. Although time in the Afterlife is more of a conceptual thing than an assurance. Days pass unmarked except by the loosest idea of a schedule. Yes, Threads of Fate is at three o'clock, standard Death Time, but days and days of three o'clocks run into one another like friends at a corner on their daily constitutional.

After a while, the coincidence becomes annoying.

That said, it was two more three o'clocks after the last three o'clock that we saw Eurydice and Penelope. It was then that Eurydice finally had what she asked for, what she'd been waiting for. And like many things in her life (and in many people's lives), it came along just as she didn't expect--but she probably should have foreseen.

Most humans (and also most ghosts) are terrible at noticing things.

Eurydice sits in Threads of Fate, measuring out yet another poor soul's deeds before deciding when, ultimately, this particular poor soul will die (and how, that's the tricky part). This one particularly tragic. Blessed with all the gifts of beauty and health and intelligence, this man is cursed with terrible luck. Always a few weeks too late for this opportunity, always a few minutes too late for the train or bus. Birds will use him for target practice, his birthday gifts will forever be belated.

And, as Eurydice measures this out, she wonders once more if this man's moods worsen more and more due to his circumstances more than his deeds. This is when Penelope (the weaver, the way) hears her best friend's muttering and leans over Eurydice's desk.

Penelope sees the usual look of confusion on Eurydice's face. The weight of a hundred Threads of Fate classes come down on Eurydice, right then. Or would have, if she weren't a ghost. Penelope has a terrific imagination, and she (unlike most humans and ghosts) is good at noticing things.

She glances at the unlucky man's thread. She sees his terrible string of luck and his terrible string of moods and reaches out, placing her own hand on top of Eurydice's arm. "Hey," she says. "You know, a man can't help his luck, but you know what he can help?"

"What?" Eurydice asks. Her eyes wide and wet and wondering.

"He can help what he does with it."

Eurydice looks down, measuring out inaction and inaction. Misdeed and misdeed. After refusal to change his circumstances, after taking out his frustration on his friends, his loved ones, on inanimate objects on strangers. It becomes too much. Sometimes other people's problems are just too much. Even for Eurydice. Even for the fates or we gods.

She picks up the scissors and cuts the thread.

She cuts the thread just as she feels the familiar chill of the class instructor looming over her.

"Good choice," they say. "You're getting better at this, Eurydice. We all learn in our own ways; you learn through your feelings and also your friends." Their ephemeral hood nods toward Penelope, who is on her second thread of the day. "Now, if you'll do me a favor and review this thread next."

"But it's already cut?" Eurydice says.

The instructor seems to smile, or is that Eurydice's imagination? None of the Instructors have faces and would be identical except in height and in voice and in build. The Threads of Fate instructor is short with spindly limbs and must have enjoyed a beer or five a night when they were alive. Their voice is deep and sonorous with a hint of echo—they'd been a long time dead and a long time an instructor (so says the echo).

Still faceless and featureless, Eurydice hears a smile when they say, "That is because this thread is yours."

And with a swish of dust on the floor, the instructor glides away like Eurydice's ghost hands glide to pick up her fate thread and look over her deeds and misdeeds. Her own action and inaction. Her own gifts and doses of luck.

I will tell you this, Eurydice was just as surprised as I was to find out that her thread did not end at her death. No. It ended after. Long after.

A trick of fate? A cruel twist? No, a play on words if I may: a good ghoul's work is never done.

EURYDICE:

MEMORIES

I had lost a bit of myself in Andi, a bit of myself in my music, but when Andi said what they said, I realized I didn't lose too much of myself in Orpheus. That wasn't it at all. No, I'd given too much of myself away. Freely, willingly, happily, thinking that it'd been a fair exchange. That I was getting back equal parts. That we were partners, lovers, equal share.

But like the piano keys: I was more light than darkness.

And just like Aristaeus had done to Orpheus, Orpheus had turned me into him.

He took so much of me, all that I'd given him, all that I portioned over in quarters and eighths, and he made it his. Because, the fact was, when he turned up at my recitals, the talk wasn't about my music, it was about: "Who the fuck just threw those black roses on the stage and disappeared?"

He'd made himself into a mystery, even though he was nothing but. The whispers that followed after my recital left the Hall with him. Following him out. They wanted to know more about Orpheus, not about me. Those same people at my recitas were also at Orpheus's at Aristaeus's. They were at their gigs; hovering outside their practice room (as it truly was theirs at this point— His & His).

He was not only the star of the music department but the star of my relationship. Whereas I hung back like a shadow, an echo that existed in his music. My music now echoed his. Was that what I was to him? To him and Aristaeus? They were using me.

Or was I using them?

This was some Mozart/Salieri type shit. But which one of us was which?

I know this: Orpheus played himself to be seen. He had to be the main attraction, bigger than Zeus even. He stole my fury and fire, he adopted it, appropriated it, made it his. The what-the-fuckery of Shostakovich with the drama of Gustav Holst that I had held so dear to my own work? It was exactly what people started talking about in *Orpheus's* compositions.

Not mine. Not mine.

Because no one was talking about me. Not anymore. And you know what? I don't think they ever were. At least, in the stories, they never mentioned me as a musician, as the inspiration for Orpheus's work. I was just another pretty face, a woman to be desired, to be sought after. Blah blah blah. But no. He was a musical lamprey.

I had to get rid of him, and fast. He'd stolen my music, my livelihood, my everything. Everything I ever wanted. My mother, on the phone told me I was being dramatic, that I was only a sophomore, that there was time to change my major to something more practical. "Your life isn't ruined, sweetie," she said. "You have years in front of you." Funny that.

Mom was right about one thing: "Eurydice, you still have your integrity, and your scholarship. You can't let anyone take either away from you."

Also? I still had Andi. And no one was going to take them away from me either.

My mother was right. The scholarship was for music, though, and I didn't want to make music anymore if it was just going to be stolen through the wall. So, I moped around, hands in pockets for a week. Sex became mechanical with both Andi and Orpheus. Ice cream tasted like cold milk, Diet Coke like seltzer. Everything was grey to me, all in clouds, all perpetual *mood*.

I didn't know yet that I'd yet lose everything to Orpheus. Everything. And, by everything, I mean my entire fucking life. So yeah, he had to go. Unfortunately, he didn't go soon enough.

Cause breakups are hard. Not only in the timing but the doing, and especially with someone I thought was supposed to be my collaborator but instead was just a gods-damned thief. I was in Andi's room, naked. My pale-as-shit legs tangled up with their own golden ones, their painted toes tickling the underside of my feet. Their muscled arm wrapped around mine so that their lavender deodorant slightly overpowered me.

"So," they said, tucking my magenta hair behind my ear. "How're you gonna do it? Cause I have some ideas."

"I have some ideas, too," I said, untucking my hair and sitting up.

They grabbed a cigarette, their chest and stomach still sweaty from the sex of twenty minutes ago. The room still smelling of it, that sweet musky smell that took a shower and a scrubbing to get off my face. I leaned back on the wall, letting one leg dangle over the edge of the metal frame bed.

"Get this," I said. "So you know how he still comes and throws those roses on stage?"

"Yeah," Andi said and exhaled a long plume of blue smoke on the filthy sheets.

"Well. I'm gonna keep playing. I have a recital coming up where I play two pieces instead of just one." I leaned in, grabbing Andi's cigarette from their mouth and taking a drag. "Anyway, I won't tell him about the extra piece. He doesn't like to

be caught off guard. And I'll announce the title of
the second piece as he's trying to leave the hall."

Andi took their smoke back from me.

"Yeah? And what is it. The title."

"Oh, it's something I've been working on for
a while, but it'll get him."

I pulled my knees up to my chest and looked
out the window at the frost forming on the pane.
Winter, dawning of a new season. An unforgiving
season, which I had to be, had to become. I was
going to come into this season with a bluster that
was gonna knock Orpheus off his feet.

"I'll get him," I said, leaning my smiling chin
on my knees. "I'll twist his fucking strings."

THE AFTERLIFE:
PRESENT DAY

Fate is a tricky thing, something Eurydice had learned over and over again in her efforts every day from three to four o'clock. Something Penelope had tried to teach her, something she had tried and tried (yet continually failed) to learn. But now, looking at her own fate thread, Eurydice is seeing something she never saw before.

She is seeing that her current circumstances are due to action and inaction, a misplaced footing here, a wrong turn there. The trick of Fate is action, the death of Fate is inaction. And how did Eurydice die? Well, that would be spoiling things, wouldn't it?

She saw her death, clearly marked in her thread, but it wasn't *The End*. We've discussed that. No, her thread continued long after that, and she saw so much inaction after that, so many missteps and mulling about, so much potential wasted. As she pores over the thread, carrying it in her hands like water, she sees new hints and possibilities. But only if she acts, if she *does* do something besides moon about and wonder aloud. Besides walk through empty parks beside her best friend. Besides wonder what to do about Orpheus's constant and (still) continual prayers.

As the bell tolls, and it always tolls in the Afterlife, ringing souls to their next task and their next contemplation, Eurydice passes Penelope on her way to the instructor.

The instructor who still waits for her. Because, unlike Eurydice, they know what Fate holds.

"Can I keep this?" Eurydice asks. "Or borrow it? Hold onto it for a little while?"

"Of course," the instructor says in their echoing voice. The scent of false promises and failed futures thick on them like AXE Body Spray. "It is your own thread, after all. I would not have given it to you if I did not mean for you to keep it." They lean in, hood hanging over their empty face. Empty breath whispering into Eurydice's ear. "Simply promise me this, that you'll do well by it. That you won't waste the opportunity I've given to you."

She looks down at the shimmering gold in her hand, shining and delicate. She's still holding it like water, like it might drip and disappear from her hands at any moment.

"How do I keep it?" Eurydice asks.

"That is up to you," the instructor says rather than asks.

Eurydice realizes that she is unsure she is ready to hold onto such a heavy thing: an entire life.

So, I had my plan. My recital plan: the one that involved Orpheus and his roses; the one that involved me playing a song arranged specifically to mock him. One written especially against him, taking everything that he loved and making it better.

Because I was better; it was time he knew that.

I'd been composing it for weeks (weeks and weeks and weeks). Practicing it when I knew Orpheus wasn't next door or outside. When I knew he was in classes or at some party or another. When I figured his friends could and would keep him occupied.

It was clear what I was, always should've been clear. I was second: second thought, second place, second chair to whatever plans or options Orpheus always had going on. Why though? Cause Aristaeus could talk to Orpheus about music on his own level. A pretentious ridiculous *high art* level that made my eyes roll across the table.

Aristaeus was the kind of intense that Orpheus liked, where I was (*was*) not.

When I was in their practice room last week, it was clear Aristaeus wasn't a shadow like me. His intensity was hot enough to burn holes in my brain. He was a real pretentious pomposter, unlike the majority of Orpheus's friends who just talked a good pretentious game but then like, majored in Finance but minored in Composition. Aristaeus put his actions behind his bullshit philosophy. Where I was the clarinet; Aristaeus was cannon fire.

Whatever Aristaeus was for Orpheus, I couldn't keep up. I'd be practicing something or other in the room I liked and I'd hear screaming from down the hall, on the regular. Not scheduled, not perfectly timed, but it was Aristaeus again. Once again, getting into an argument over his nihilistic stance on fucking everything. He'd been escorted from the music building once for the destruction of property (knocking an EXIT sign down in a rage), and now he was more chill about his screaming matches.

Marginally.

At least he kept Orpheus busy so that I could work on my "surprise." So that I could compose the most Jerry Lee Lewisesque, rockabilly rendition of one of his pieces. A piano-pop explosion of everything he rallied against in his own work, in my work, in any musical work.

According to Orpheus (and Aristaeus), popularity was the death of art. Art should make one feel things, he often said. Not sing along, not dance. It should sink into one's bones and cause them to stand on edge; to be confused.

I always thought dancing and singing along meant someone was feeling things. Call me a weirdo. Shrug emoji.

Dancing and singing along was exactly what I had in mind when I sat down at the piano for my recital. That fateful recital, the final one of the winter semester. Not Aristaeus and his fanaticism, although it should have been. Not Andi and the way they loved me, although that should probably have been as well. No, the only thing I thought of was revenge.

Revenge, as the wide and cold auditorium filled up with people, one of them Andi, none of them Aristaeus. As the smell of damp increased with trodden-in snow and wet coats from the inches upon inches piling up outside. The auditorium was a respite from exams and the cold. A waystation on the way to the cafeteria from one side of campus to the other, and also another hope at a glimpse of Orpheus's theatrics.

With its tall and rounded ceilings and its creaky narrow gum-soaked seats, it was a poor excuse of a respite, but the acoustics were great. I could hear every footstep, every wet cough, every stifled giggle, every tappity tap tap of the unsilenced speed-texting afficionados.

Even though I knew these people were here to hear me, I was going to play for Orpheus alone. Not for my instructors' jury sat at the front, looking up at me: not only my personal instructor, currently peering over his glasses. But the other instructors also; their pens poised like conductor batons over their clipboards. They, too, hated anticipation.

With a sigh disguised as a deep breath, I drowned out the smells and sound (the mildew, the creaking seats, and someone pacing backstage) and placed my cold and aching fingers on the starting keys. My shoulders shook as the breath exhaled, but still, my hands were on the right keys. It was time to begin: Rachmaninov's "Prelude in G Minor."

A rather silly and ridiculously easy piece for me, I knew, but this recital was about the performance, not the skill. About two minutes in, at the hard rests and half-waltz, I stuck my tongue out the side of my mouth. A mockery of the piece and of myself. Then quickly retracting it into a serene smile as my body swayed with the tidelike quietesse of the notes that proceeded the silly plodding toddler-like musicality.

Continuing the performance aspect of the

recital, I sighed heavily moving my entire torso with the grandiosity that Rachmaninov required. The audience, however, sat politely unmoved. The sniffles and coughs continued, the rat-a-tat of the texting punctuated the ebb and flow of the piece. The going from beauty to hardship one after the other. But I had to keep going. Silence was death, stopping at this point was, in hindsight a good idea.

I was, however, a woman with one thing on her mind: fucking over Orpheus.

This was a farce of a recital, Rachmaninov's Prelude not only a joke of a piece for my skill, but a pun: it was a prelude of what was yet to come. Not only in my performance, but what was to become of Orpheus. Orpheus, who I knew was out there. I saw him sneak in, just as my instructors gestured for me to begin. His black, high-collared coat silhouette outlined in bright winter light and a rush of snow. He always had to be dramatic.

Rachmaninov's final notes flourished as they always did: a dramatic cannon fire of destruction. I stood as I played them, spinning on my heels to take what these thirteen in the audience must (might) assume was my final bow. But it wasn't, as I knew, as my instructors knew.

There was a slight pause after the bow. My instructors made their notations, and the audience eventually rose from their seats with a rustle of coats to give an appropriately polite (yet muffled mittened) applause. Yet still, I stood. I had to wait. Wait the allotted amount of time for Orpheus to make his grand gesture; his predictable gesture.

And predictably, he did. Right on time, too.

The roses landed at my feet with the sort of accuracy of someone who's been practicing this move in his dorm room. But I did not do as I normally did and stand stunned, staring at the roses and Orpheus's grand exit. No. This time I swooped down and held the roses aloft for a brief moment before setting them down on the piano bench, where I also sat, and took to the keys once more.

The music I played struck Orpheus right in his heart and wrong in his ear.

It was the opening to my favorite piece of his: "Haunt of Birds in G Minor," yet with my own Eurydice twist. I'd taken out all the pretention Orpheus loved and added all the danceability he hated, making his own music into a farce of itself. Less than a minute in, I had the audience tapping their feet and my instructors' tapping their pens. And Orpheus? He was stuck stock still with fists at his side, totally undone.

I continued my performance, a true fury on the keys. My fingers assaulted the high notes, alighting on the heavy ones: contrast in light and darkness, the way Orpheus never expected us to be, or his music to be. I had turned his *high art* into a radio hit. Anyone could dance to it. How dare.

Thing was? I couldn't stop smiling. This new face of Orpheus's music was an anathema to him. To him and Aristaeus and their entire philosophy on music. It ripped this piece from the hands of the *elite* and gave it to people who just wanna have fun.

The true lovers of music: everyone else.

It didn't matter what they thought, though. Not to me. What did Orpheus think? It was evident in his posture: rigid as a Venetian statue in the aisle, fists clenched, jaw sculpted in rage as I neared the end of his (formerly) six-minute masturbatory distortion fest, that I'd turned into a three-and-a-half-minute piano bop.

Me though? I not only nearing the end of the song, but the end of my ability to deal. Sweat poured down my face, down my shirt, and pooled in my shoes. My breathing came heavy and hot in my throat and lungs, bile rising in my throat, all of me stinging from the nerves of the performance and the anticipation of Orpheus's reaction.

I thought by now I'd be tasting victory.

But victory, I'd find out, would come much, much later.

As the final bars hit and my hair stuck to my face and the metallic taste of fear coated my tongue. I worried about three things: that my fingers would slip; that my resolve would slip; or that my plan would slip. But I also knew this. I knew this arrangement like I knew the curves of Andi's hips and their lips. This arrangement would not betray me.

Only Orpheus would.

The last notes pound with a flip back of my soaked hair and a spin of my heels. I held my arms high for an exaggerated bow. This time? This time the applause from the audience was real, felt. They screamed and stomped their feet. Cheered and jumped up and down. This was true appreciation. I knew this, because not once did they sit back down. Not once in those sweat-soaked, fury-soaked, three-plus minutes.

The storm was not over. Because my reason for worry was real. Because Orpheus was climbing the stairs. He was applauding as well, cheering and screaming. Calling my name louder and bigger than any of the crowd who'd come in actually to hear me. Andi among them, starting a chant: "Eur-Y-Dic-E!" over and over.

I was frozen. Staring at him with my sweat gone cold as he rushed me, threw his arms around me, and held me high, like a principal ballerina. His smile as he did this was untrue, unkind, he knew what I was doing, what I had done. There was a plot, a plan behind his intent. The metallic taste of my mouth grew sour, bitter. My stomach twisted and turned.

When he set me down, his gaze turned to adoration. I threw up a little in my mouth, but I saved the vomit for later. *Don't throw up, Eurydice,* I told myself. *Don't fuck this up.* I told myself as Orpheus got down on one knee and everything then got sent to my brain in small bits and bites. The room went silent except for the roaring between my ears, all this, I guess, helped me focus on what the hell was going on because.

Because.

He fucking got down on one knee and pulled a small box out of his pocket and said.

He said.

"Eurydice, you talented woman, you light and love of my life."

He said.

"Will you marry me?"

And then? That's when I threw up.

AFTERLIFE:
PRESENT DAY

Jealousy is a terrible predator and something we gods are guilty of. Gods are predators, as you very well know. Mortals are quite aware of the way the divine play with their lives by now, at least some of them. Those that cast their lot at dice or cards or in places of worship scream Why! at the top of their lungs when they do not get their way. While others yet are blessed over and over with the turn of a card or the turn of a phrase.

It is not our fault.

Although technically, it is.

We have favorites, and can you blame us? Even in my domain, where I am not allowed to interfere with mortal lives, my wife is immune. In her six months where she walks the mortal plane, she can interfere as much as she likes. And while in her eternity of godhood, she's done so once before, she found another recent mortal life very intriguing.

She took a liking to Eurydice very well.

Persephone is said to be mercurial like the seasons, but the seasons have no such mercurial intent. They are organized and have their plans: fallow, birth, life, death. Is it any wonder that such an organized goddess with such a long view would take kindly to Eurydice? A woman with similar views? Women like Eurydice and goddesses like Persephone stick together.

This is something I have known for quite some time.

And something a devoted husband never objects to.

Persephone returned to me one cooling evening and said, "This one, Eurydice, I want to talk to her when she comes to us. That all right with you?"

And I turned to her and said, "Of course, you may, my love. She is terribly wronged, as you once were. It only makes sense that it would be you, my dear, my sweet, who would teach this songbird that there is a *Coda* after the *Fin*."

My beautiful wife smiled at me then, and we watched the story of Eurydice and Orpheus play out. We did not interfere when the awful and terrible Aristaeus became involved. A young man who'd already gained a reputation for playing favorites and cruel jealousy, as well as a penchant for pushing anyone (and everyone) out of his way to get what he wants.

However, my wife will do the same.

The seasons are pretty brutal, don't you know?

I tend not to get involved in mortal lives. It is not my place, as I have been told over and over. I was told: *Hades, you have ultimate power, once the mortal's life has ended. Otherwise, you do nothing.* So, I do nothing until death. Then, I provide for them a place to prove themselves, to judge them or allow them to ascend or descend accordingly.

Persephone, though? She is her own woman. A good husband does not control his wife. A good relationship is one of equals, where the partners recognize the strengths of the other or others. Where the partners allow them to play out and complement one another.

This is why Persephone and I last in bliss while the other gods quarrel.

So, when Eurydice had her Fate Thread lovingly spooled up in her pocket, while she worried the ends over and over in her fingers during Hauntings Class, while her instructor said to her again and again, "Eurydice, you are too *seen.* You are too *noticed.* Be less than yourself. Be less you." While the Instructor said this, Eurydice drew into herself with her thoughts (which was not being less her at all).

"Be less me," she says to Penelope yet another identical grey day over yet another cardamom tea.

"Be less you," Penelope parrots back. Her

fingers tap like spiders' legs over her cup. "Like that's even possible? You're great, as you are"

"But the instructor wants that, and I want to haunt Orpheus."

Penelope frowns, turning to look at a ghost of a woman behind them who is speaking to her ghost friend about her leftover family. She turns back, worry wrought on her waning face. Penelope is due to go Beyond soon.

"Okay, bear with me a moment." Penelope chews on her lips, a gesture that meant something at one time. "What if you're not supposed to haunt Orpheus? What if Orpheus is supposed to haunt you?"

Eurydice thinks about this. With the barrage of messages that continue to arrive and how she cannot stop thinking about him day after day, hour after hour, due to his consistent badgering, it is true, Penelope is right: Orpheus *is* haunting her.

She pulls her Fate Thread from her pocket and looks at it for the sixth time that day, but this time she studies it like she's reading a book that requires critical thinking.

Penelope smiles, thin and sad.

"I mean, I'm still haunted by Odysseus. So it seemed legit to say, except Odysseus is dead and, okay, maybe not so legit."

Except totally legit.

Because Penelope knows a thing or two about being haunted by the ghost of legendary men.

She sips her own tea, looking up at the grey and infinite sky. She is meant to go Beyond, to weave the tapestries of Fate. She hasn't told Eurydice. Not yet. She doesn't even know if she's going to; she's afraid the news might ruin her.

How poorly we know our friends.

The pause lingers, and when Eurydice looks up, she's confused.

"Oh," she says. "It's weird. There's an unevenness left behind, and that means." She looks down again. "You're one hundred percent right."

EURYDICE:
MEMORIES

Surprisingly, Orpheus took me out to dinner despite the spectacle.

Two days later though, after he'd cooled off and done a load of laundry and a lot of keening duets with Aristaeus. Orpheus and I were sitting across from each other in a diner booth (I made sure our knees, our feet, none of us touched). My nails bit into the greasy, faux leather booth cushion as I stared at him, willing him (daring him) not to ask me to marry him again. I'd been having nightmares about it. It'd been occupying my every waking thought.

My instructor even told me to go to the Counseling Center cause my anxiety was making him anxious. That helped me not at all. I didn't know anxiety was contagious.

Dreams come true, as they say. So do, unfortunately, nightmares. The waitress didn't even have time to come around and offer drinks, or even set down silverware before Orpheus tried again. The table was bare between us, save for a swath of winter sunshine that split the table in two. Harsh, like I should've been.

"I'm serious, Eurydice," he said. "I want to marry you."

I pretended to take two long yoga breaths. I've never done yoga, but I've watched some on YouTube. After the second exhale, I said.

"I know." It was all I could say.

The answer in my heart, the answer that was screaming in my head was *No. Fuck off. Fuck off for a million years, Orpheus.* But the answer that I'd been conditioned to say from a hundred thousand rom-coms, by my parents, and by all twelve spectators' fast-spreading gossip was: *Yes, a million times yes.*

"And?" he asked.

It was all he could say.

Two more pretend yoga breaths, a glance around the room, a grip and regrip on the faux leather cushion. I could only stall for so long. Ten seconds went by. Twenty. Then I looked Orpheus right in the eyes. I conjured up everything I knew about weddings, about engagements, about Orpheus. Everything gleaned from family movie night and Reality TV with my sisters. Thought about everything he and I had been through together, weighed my heart on all that, looked at him and said, "Yes," but then immediately opened my mouth to say, *No.*

It was too late. No take-backsies at this point, cause Orpheus was already on one knee, the box was open, and the carved silver band was going on my finger. The carved silver band I'd been oohing over on Etsy, it currently had my mouth hanging open and the waitress' mouth too, and the bartenders' and, and, and.

Orpheus smiled at me. Perfect execution.

"Will you marry me, Eurydice?" he asked.

Now it was too embarrassing to say what I wanted to say. We had an audience. This was a performance piece now. I could take it back later. Probably?

"Yes," I said.

Then came the kiss and offers for drinks on the house and I don't even remember what happened next except that I had a spinach salad so wilted that it should have been obvious foreshadowing

I only remember what happened after we left the diner.

We went back to his room and the door was barely shut before we were pulling off each other's clothes; we newly minted fiancés. Clothes ended up on the floor, on the bedrail, on his desk and we finally, actually fucked.

We fucked like he meant it for the first time. And for the first time with Orpheus, I came. He looked at me like he'd done some sort of magic, like he didn't know what was happening, but he came right after, without warning.

Later when we were lying on the bed, sweating in the radiator heat and sharing a cigarette, he looked at me. Looked at me for real-real like he was trying to figure me out; as if the person he thought he had figured out this entire time was false. And let's be real, his version of me was false. He'd been using me like a musical ATM this entire time.

"Was that an actual orgasm?" he said.

Oh shit. I gave the cigarette back to stare at the ceiling.

"Well," I lied. "They've all been actual orgasms, this one was just." I continued to lie. "I was *really* into it."

He turned to me and wrapped his arm around me. He was getting hard again against my leg. My breathing came shallow as my heartbeats as his hair fell across my face; his whisper hot in my ear. "I'll make a wife out of you yet," he said.

And oh gods, we fucked again. And I came again.

Not ashamed to admit.

The ring sat on the bedroom table the next morning in the early dawn light, casting a long shadow of itself across the ashes. I awoke sticky and sore in a miasma of stale smoke and stale sex. Orpheus was already gone. A note taped to his computer: *BBL.*

What business he had at six in the morning I figured happened at four in the morning and probably was an Aristaeus booty call. Both those men had libidos like car batteries, they went and went and went until they died. And then it took a heated argument to get them started again.

I saw it three weeks ago across the bar having drinks with Andi. Watching the two men sullen next to each other in our shared booth. Andi and I'd left 'cause Orpheus and Aristaeus were fighting over who was a better composer Glenn Branca or Michael Gira.

"Too pretentious for me," Andi said. "Let's move."

The two of us hung out, elbows on the bar, listening to Taylor Swift in our ears and in our chests and drowning out any potential conversation or interaction except I was people-watching (Andi was texting Hector). And the people we were watching were Orpheus and Aristaeus, who were arguing hotter and hotter until their hands were on one-another's hands, and then their lips were on one another's lips, and then the whole bar was *Woo-hoo!ing* them on.

As Andi and I followed them home on paved paths littered with pine needles. All four of us in winter coats. All of our breaths making clouds, all of us with gloves and boots and hats against the late-November air. Andi and I wore mittens, our hands clasped together as we watched Orpheus and Aristaeus gesture wildly with thin leather gloves that went with their aesthetic. They were ten, then twenty feet ahead of us.

We let them walk away. As they faded into the December late night, Andi whispered in my ear. They said, "Aristaeus is the jealous type, I heard." They then stopped on the road, so I stopped, both of us pulling off our mittens to light cigarettes and seek shelter from the wind. "Jealous and mean about it too."

(This was before the recital plan, this was before the proposal, this was before the actual fucking and the ring and everything that would come after.)

Andi put their hand on my cheek as they exhaled to the side. Then they dropped the three words that change a relationship forever. They either sent me running away or running toward someone. With Andi, they sent me running to them, listening to them, believing them.

They said.

"I love you, Eurydice," they exhaled. Hard. The words sapped them. "Fuck, I never said that to you before, but I really, really love you."

"I love you too, Andi," I said.

"Do you though?" They searched my face, looking for the lie. Their cold thumb traced my cheekbone. "Do you really? Or are you just parroting back to me what I said like you parrot back everything to Orpheus. I want you to feel things for real. For *real*, Eurydice."

"I do feel things?" I said. Asked? Said.

They exhaled again and then took my face in both their freezing hands.

"Then feel this."

They kissed me. Their long black smoke and coconut conditioner hair falling over my face and I breathed them in. Every minute and every breath. Their fingers went into my own greasy hair and pulled off my hat, their callouses tumbling through my hair, their bitten nails catching, snagging.

But I didn't mind. I was too caught up in them.

In this.

And as suddenly as it began, it ended.

"Did you feel that?" they asked

"Yeah." My breath and knees were weak. The word came out shaking.

"Do you love me, Eurydice?"

"Yes, I love you," I said. And I meant it.

Andi placed a jagged nail on my nose and smiled.

"Good."

THE AFTERLIFE:
PRESENT DAY

At three o'clock Standard Death Time, Eurydice must attend mandatory Threads of Fate sewing lessons. However, the Instructor does not expect Eurydice today. In fact, he so much does not expect her, that he wrote to her six o'clock Hauntings Instructor and to excuse Eurydice from the class.

"She is otherwise engaged," the Threads of Fate Instructor writes, with his inconsequential hand, a rather consequential note.

When the Hauntings Instructor receives this, he arrives at my door at eleven o'clock Standard Death Time. Mornings and evenings do not matter in the Afterlife. Time scarcely matters; it is simply a means for convenience to keep things running smoothly for those new souls who have not quite adjusted to reality.

The reality that time is fake.

Still yet, the Hauntings Instructor arrives at

my door. Which is not as guarded as legends say. Cerberus is a guard dog indeed, but one must be an extremely nasty soul to be fed to his jaws, and Persephone and I are very careful when deciding who has a nasty soul and who does not. *Sisyphus-Got-What-He-Deserved.*

Persephone opens the door with her usual way, a sweep of her hand and a swish of her skirts and hair as she waves the Instructor in. She says in her deep husky voice (deep with seasons and sounding like autumn), "Oh good, it's you." Her hand drops to her side as she pats Cerberus up from his nap to come to her side. "We're in the hall. Come join us."

The Hauntings Instructor is falsely confident as always when they arrive in front of me. I need to destroy that confidence not because I want to but because it is expected of me, and it would be awful not to live up to someone's expectations. Rude even.

So of course, I raise my (empty) chalice to them and say, "Why yes, it is you! I half expected you not to show. We redid the labyrinth yesterday, but you are so clever. I always did say they were so clever, didn't I, Persephone?"

"You did, dear, yes," she says, placing her hand on my pale, bare knee.

"Now." I lean forward, face covered in a shroud as it always is, at all times in The Hall. My dark hair hangs over my shoulders in an appearance of unwashed grease and ephemera. But this is only for show. "What is it you wanted again?"

My voice booms and echoes the way only a god's voice can. It is the sound of winter's bleakest moments, turned to Celsius. While I lean forward, my grey elbows on my grey knees, Persephone leans back. Her own rosy skin paling from the underground dim, her hair blond and curly (and shining). Her lips are red with pomegranate, her fingers, too.

She smiles a full set of stained teeth.

"I wanted," the Hauntings Instructor says or begins. "I wanted to know why the student Eurydice is permitted to skip class. In all my eternity under your employ, I have never had a student permitted to 'skip' class. Much less with permission from the Threads of Fate Instructor."

I turn back, glancing at Persephone. She is winding a curl around her longest finger. The middle one, for clarity.

"Eurydice is a special case," she says.

She is not looking at him. She is looking at a stalactite.

It is my turn to speak. "Leave the soul to us. We will take her instruction from this point on."

If a shadow inside an idea of a robe could shiver, the Hauntings Instructor does. They shiver and clasp their insubstantial hands three times (and three different ways), turning their hood this way and that.

"I see. Ah. Well then." A pause where only distant lapping of water can be heard. "A demigod it is to be?"

Persephone's voice is an entire smile. "You'll see."

"I'll, I'll see? You're sending me away with that?"

"Indeed," I say, also smiling. "You'll see. Now go."

And they did. Immediately.

EURYDICE:

MEMORIES

Orpheus and I were now engaged. Andi and I were weeks in love. Let's face it, Orpheus and I weren't in love, we weren't even in lust. He wanted to collect me and place me underneath him, both in the bedroom and in his career. With my display at the recital, when I made his music into a mockery of his own ideology, I became exactly what he feared.

I was better than him, and he knew it.

He had a plan. Like he said: *I'll make a wife out of you yet.*

What he wasn't predicting, and what I knew about, was Andi. Andi and their perfect way of loving, appreciating, and knowing me. They understood me in a way Orpheus didn't, and never ever would. And I suppose this is why Orpheus collected Aristaeus to him, because Aristaeus worshipped and complimented him in a way I never ever would and never ever could.

Aristaeus was bad news. Not only did he worship and compliment the worst parts of Orpheus, he also built them up like a crescendo. The two of them becoming louder and louder in their elitist rhetoric and uncomfortable philosophy that whenever I hung out in their practice room now, I texted Andi or Hector to come and knock on the door to "rescue" me. Once Orpheus and I got engaged, rather than growing closer, I distanced myself: bit by bit, step by step, refrain by refrain.

Andi was lying on the rickety spare (yet still here) piano bench in my practice room, reading over an Econ paper while I practiced Liszt. They appreciated Liszt paired with Economics. They always said the two went together: overly complex with simple solutions that fucked everyone over.

They looked up at me when I hit the final notes.

"Okay, that was good stuff." Swinging their legs over the edge of the bench, they sat up and brushed stray long hairs out of their face. "I gotta go give Hector some attention before he freaks the shit out. Do you mind waiting here for like twenty? Thirty minutes?"

"Not at all," I smiled, kissing them quickly before they went to the door. "Say hi to him for me."

I grinned and leaned back, vice grip on my own piano bench as Andi left the practice room, getting a new pack of smokes ready. While they were gone, I arranged my own composition pages, something

I'd been working on for weeks. Since before the recital, before the proposal, before Aristaeus.

Something a little poppy-boppy-you-can-dance-to-it fun times.

Before totally switching gears (Lizt to Liberace needed a little doomscrolling), I checked my phone for messages: another Zeus meme from mom. Social media notifications: someone on Twitter yelling about stuff. And then did my doomscrolling until someone knocked on the door. It'd only been five or six minutes. Andi wouldn't be back this fast. And when they entered, it wasn't Andi back this fast.

It was Aristaeus.

"Hey," he said in his over-dramatic way of always looking and sounding like a Joy Division album cover.

I had to try not to be shocked. I had to try to be expecting him. But I know I failed 'cause three composition pages fell to the floor in my attempt to be casual as my elbow swept over the piano and onto the high keys with a discordant plunk that both he and Orpheus would adore.

"Oh hey," I said. "Good to see you."

"Is it?" he said. He said as he swept over to the rickety piano bench, sitting down perfectly posed and collected, the way he did everything. He was here with an agenda and also somehow bored at the same time. His warped hoodie sleeve fell off his shoulder, revealing the snake head tattooed on his arms, the fangs on his fingers, and the coil of its body around his neck.

He used the fangs to brush back his too-messy hair in a unobtrusive and noticeable way, like a statue.

"It is," I said in a way convincing him that it totally was not.

"Good." He smiled a bored smile and leaned his knees on his elbows, folding his fingers together, but his gaze stayed on me. That intense gaze that I knew had drawn Orpheus in like he could fill that space. "I'm here to talk about Andi."

"What." I paused. I wasn't ready for this. "What about them?"

"They're not good for you," Aristaeus said. "You know this. I know this. Orpheus knows this. But Andi doesn't know this." He sighed, leaning back on the bench in a way it really shouldn't allow but somehow did. "They're not good for your career, Eurydice. They're steering you wrong."

"Wrong."

The word hit the air like off-time Tchaikovsky cannon fire.

"Wrong," he echoed. "You and Orpheus are the real deal. A duo for the ages. He's the Ike to your Tina; you're the Kim to his Thurston."

(I couldn't help but notice the problematic pairings.)

Aristaeus ran his tongue over his top lip in both a pensive and hungry way, as if the thought itself was delicious. "Andi is a complication. They have to go."

"Go," I said. Saying one word for the second time.

"Yes, go."

"I don't understand," I said because I didn't. But I did, but in Aristaeus's terms, a man of dramatic means, I was afraid of what *Go* meant. Aristaeus was calm, too calm. Like how right before a storm when the whole world gets scared and stops moving for a second cause nature's trying to explain to you that the shit's about to go down? That was Aristaeus right now.

"They have to go. Somewhere where they never come back."

The words were dark, as they were meant to be. The fluorescents buzzed appropriately and too dramatically, punctuating the point. My own now-bitten nails crunched into the worn wood of my piano bench, splintering it further. My stomach tied and cinched itself so that I became two inches shorter, hunching toward Aristaeus like a predator, but instead, I was just in pain.

I wanted to stand. I wanted to stand and tell Aristaeus to get out. To get out and go somewhere where he could never come back. I wanted to strike his perfect chest and rake my decrepit nails through his perfect skin.

This was the first time I ever truly hated someone. The first.

"What do you want me to do?" I said.

"Nothing," Aristaeus said, rising from the piano bench. "I'll take care of it. I have a plan."

Now I stood. I stood and rushed over to him, grabbing him by his over-crusted shirt collar and searching his expression as if I could find some truth (any truth) in it. I held him there as he looked at me with neither fear nor defiance.

The pomposity washed off him like a smell: Obsession. A cologne with a total absence of humanity. His hair was too styled, not because he never washed it, but because he had all the time in the world to tend to it. He was the portrait of irony and pretention because he *was* both; he could *be* both, because cultivated both into an aesthetic. And aesthetics was all Aristaeus cared about. I had to do one thing and one thing only.

Let go. There was no way I was getting through to this guy.

No way.

"A plan," I said.

My voice small and afraid, but trying to be big. Like a piccolo.

"Yes," he said, brushing off his shirt where I'd held it. "Now, if you'll let me get to work."

"I—"

"Eurydice," he said.

The *Don't* was implied.

THE AFTERLIFE:
PRESENT DAY

Eurydice has no classes! How glorious. And it may have been glorious news to hear, except for the caveat the instructor brings her after the first bit of news. "Eurydice, you have no classes," an instructor she does not know tells her as she wakes up. As she blinks, only as a ghost can blink, washing away the memories of her life that she'd had upon sleeping (or what passes for sleep for a ghost).

Eurydice nods.

"I have no classes." Only then does the confusion set in. "Am I moving Beyond?"

"No," the instructor says. "It is something different. You have been summoned."

The word hits like weight. Weight is something present only in teacups and cake in the Afterlife. In things that are pleasant to hold and behold. But to Eurydice this word of *summoned* feels like a heft on her chest, one that seems burdensome rather than cake-sweet or teacup-smooth.

"I understand," she says.

Even though she does not.

As ghosts do not have to either brush teeth or do any of the mundanities of the living (something some of you have been astute enough to notice), Eurydice rises to follow this instructor to her summoning.

She travels down roads she knows, past restaurants and parks she visited with Penelope. Places where she tasted delicious teas and foods and had conversations that wrecked what was left of her heart. Then she travels roads she doesn't know. Fields of wheat that have been sown for winter, other fields that lie fallow. Skies that are winter-bleak with birds that dot them just out of reach of identification. She watches them as they watch her. The instructor does not speak, perhaps because they are not addressed by Eurydice, who follows behind with her worries and anticipations.

Which are principally and in order: *What have I done? Where am I going?* And finally: *Will I ever see Penelope again?*

The answer, unfortunately, to the last question is yes.

The answers to the other two questions are simple: Eurydice has done nothing but the correct things in the Afterlife. And as for where she is going, she is coming to visit me.

This question is answered when she gets to my door, and the realization hits her of where she is (theoretically), and where she's been (realistically). She shudders in that way that only the truth can make a person shudder, and then, the instructor leaves her.

They leave Eurydice to her worrying and hand-wringing to the dotted birds above. To the bleak wind of winter and to my godsight. But it is not for long, as it is only a moment, or several, before the door opens, and time is changed forever.

EURYDICE:

MEMORIES

The meeting with Aristaeus left me in a panic. When Andi came back, as they did, as they always did, my sheet music was already packed up in my backpack, the broken zipper fought to close and the whole thing on my back. I was standing within sight of the door, fists opening and closing.

They didn't have a chance to utter the word they were holding before I said, "We have to leave."

"Okay, leave. So, pizza or different kind of *'pizza'*?"

They were humoring me.

"No like leave-leave. Call an Uber, now, destination: get the fuck out of town."

There was hesitation, of course, there was hesitation when Andi pulled out their phone, swiped here, there, everywhere while glancing at me more than a couple times. Their finger finally hovered over the screen while their eyes read my face, my face which was required reading at this point: abject terror, a fugue in G-minor. They took a long and necessary breath before breathing, their exhale shuddering, holding back what they knew they had to say.

What they should say. And it was, "Eurydice, what the ever-living fuck is going on."

"Can't say," I said. "Tell you when we get there."

"Can I grab food first?" they asked, as they pressed: get the fuck out of town.

"I have some granola bars," I said, hand shaking as I turned the doorknob. "Let's go."

Go, that was the word for the day. Go anywhere. Go somewhere where you can't come back. Go now. Stopping was the one thing I didn't want to do. Couldn't do, that wasn't an option. Stop was the one word I didn't want to hear, was the one word that I refused to listen to. Except there were two of us, and I refused to control Andi. I couldn't even if I wanted to.

And I wouldn't.

The moment we left the music building, furtively calm (again, like a piccolo), there was a voice across the quad. "Andi!" They turned, of course, they turned. They turned with a cigarette poised in their mouth, hands cupped around their lighter. "Andi! Hey! Where're you going?"

It was Hector. He waved and ran over, in his gangly way of running over that would be expected of half the Econ majors: one half weighed down by calculators, the other half quasi-muscled businessfolk. Andi broke the mold. They always broke the mold.

"Where're you going?" Hector asked again, he repeated things a lot for emphasis.

Andi panicked. They rarely, if ever, panicked. The last time I saw Andi panic was when they had to choose between a brown or chunky red cardigan in a BOGO sale at the thrift store, and we only had cash on hand for one of them. They ended up closing their eyes and choosing the red one (ps: they still regret their choice).

"Uh. Nowhere."

Which was, technically, the truth.

"I'm coming with," Hector said. "Nowhere sounds fun."

From hanging out with Hector, I know he was picked last for everything at school on up and still carried that memory with him all the way to bed at night. Now he wanted in on Andi's and my Get Out Of Here team, and the FOMO was real. Beads of sweat were already forming at the tight black curls at his forehead and running down his worried expression that was busy trying not to look worried.

"No," I said. And I said too quickly, so quickly as to arouse suspicion.

"What do you mean, No? You two never avoid me, like ever. Unless you're up to lesbian business."

"No lesbian business." That was Andi. In an obvious We Are Trying To Avoid You answer.

"Right, well, uh, I'll just be over here. You know, not being avoided."

Hector then backed up in a way that, if he were a van, would require beeping. Slowly, tentatively, and narrowly missing stationary objects.

Andi and I hurried off to where the Uber was coming to get us, with only our backpacks and guilt weighing us down. Caught, we were caught, and we both knew by the sound of Hector's sad and ungraceful footsteps that he was worriedly following after us.

We found out that Uber ghosted us when we arrived at the Campus Designated Rideshare Pickup Spot. Andi was frantically trying to order another one 'cause I'm sure I looked like the shakiest vibrato ever to be attempted when Hector joined us. Again.

"No, seriously, where are you two going," he said, adjusting his overladen backpack. "You're being super suspicious. Very suspicious. Did you do something?"

"Nowhere," Andi said. "I mean it."

"Andi, don't say nothing, you definitely did something. Or is someone else trying to do something? Let me help you. I'm not dense."

Hector looked like he needed help himself,

as usual. His flat top looked like it was trying to do the wave, his skin looked alternately ashy and greasy at the same time and was somehow both wiry and underfed. Hector, I would find out from Andi later, basically lived on a diet of Sour Cream & Onion Chips and 7-Up and occasionally had a vegan hot dog (as a treat).

"Fine," Andi said. "You can help. Because I love you."

They shoved their backpack, which had their laptop and phone inside. All that good, delicious GPS stuff. "Take this, keep it in your room. Keep my phone on you, whenever, wherever."

"You got it?"

He did not, actually, got it.

"Don't ask questions," we both said at the same time.

"Part of the deal," Andi said.

"You got it."

Hector held out the backpack like it was something that would explode, his arms shaking with the weight. He looked at us as if we were something dangerous as well. I could almost see the second thoughts forming about the backpack, about us, about everything.

"Should I tell someone? The Dean or something?"

"No!" I said. "I mean, no."

The Dean of Students was a woman who had a penchant for starting trouble where there was none, thinking all men were pigs (except the one or two who actually *were pigs* she thought were somehow okay), and treated most women like competition. She was, in effect, a monster. Not really, but she made monsters out of all of us.

He bit his lips in that way that told me he was totally gonna tell someone.

"Hector, I love you, I need this," Andi said in that totally suspicious (not suspicious) way. "Can you just keep the phone and laptop on you? Plugged in? You can keep it in your room."

Hector nodded. "Where will you be?"

Andi and I looked at each other.

"My mom's house," Andi said. "I'm gonna get an absentee note from classes for a couple days. I'll snag the homework off the blackboard blah blah blah."

"Okay." Hector nodded conspiratorially. Like he suddenly gained the ability to be sneaky. Spoiler Alert: he did not.

"I'll call you."

But he knew that Andi's mom lived in another state. Hector was a smart guy, it didn't take a genius to figure out that if Andi was running away with me, then Andi was probably gonna be crashing with me. Gosh, we were young and obvious and oblivious. And Hector was a lot smarter than he looked.

THE AFTERLIFE:
PRESENT DAY

There are several ways to become a demigod. One of them is when a god loves a mortal very very much, and if you are an adult human, you have likely heard this tale in its entirety. Another way, and the way Eurydice will reach demigod status, is through favoritism.

If you recall, we gods play favorites.

We are cruel and capricious beings and not at all fair.

Eurydice is meant to become a demigod through the careful application of talent to a dose of her willful tenacity with a soupçon of vengeance. This, my friends, is the correct recipe for a demigod. It allows for the right application of revenge without quite the nemesis angle that one expects from the divine.

We gods are never one's nemesis.

We are too busy being one another's.

However, Eurydice knows none of this as my

stone doors sweep open to reveal Persephone standing in the bleak, dripping, echoing hallway, flanked by her loyal Cerberus. Cerberus, whose dominant head inches forth to lick Eurydice on the hand. He, like the two of us, has been expecting her. As a good guard dog does.

Is Eurydice stunned? Of course, she is, she is even more stunned as Persephone smiles one of those smiles that is sun after days of winter clouds. The sort of winter clouds that cause the cold to seep into one's bones and make everything, including houses to cry out in pain.

So, she smiles, my wife, and extends her hand.

"Eurydice," she says in a voice that sounds like summer rain. "Please come in. It would do us an honor."

And Eurydice does because very few people can resist Persephone's invitation. I watch the two women walk my entry hall with my godsight. I watch as Eurydice tries to keep her eyes on the dark pools on the floor (you know by now that the River Styx runs above us). She tries to keep her memories of Charon and the River at bay. But confusion sets in her face: *where is she? why is she here?*

Persephone can feel it, I know, as she quickens her step, calling Cerberus to her side with a pat on her hip. She folds her hair over her shoulder to watch Eurydice continue to wring her ghost hands as her attention flits from empty alcove to empty alcove. A place where trophies would be, should the Afterlife award such things to gods or those who briefly inhabit it.

But this is not a place for commendation or celebration.

This is a waystation (or a permanence for the foul).

As we enter The Hall, Persephone sweeps over to lounge beside me on the throne built for two and a half (Cerberus takes his place between us, his three heads trying to find comfort on either of our laps). Eurydice, however, stands feet apart, arms crossed over her chest. She is defiant.

"I know who you are," she says.

She says this to me of course.

"Oh?" I am amused. "And who am I?"

"Hades, God of the Afterlife."

"Very correct," I say, leaning forward, my face shrouded, hair reaching down past my shoulders, the concavity of my chest even more grotesque in this light. "Does that frighten you?"

Eurydice makes the motion of taking a breath although the gesture is both needless and empty. But her shoulders and chest heave with the effort and the effect is noticed. As she mock-exhales, she looks me where she knows my eyes are behind my shroud.

"No," she says. "It does not frighten me."

But it does, that much is evident in the shaking of her ghost-robes. In the shaking of her lip, which she now bites to keep still.

Persephone rests her hand on my knee as she leans forward. "Do not be afraid," she says. We didn't call you here to hurt you or to punish you."

"Why did you call me here."

The retort is a bark, not a bite.

"To receive a gift, Eurydice," Persephone says. "You are neither to be damned nor to be sent back. You are here because you are a great and shining soul."

"Very correct," I say as I lay my hand atop my wife's. She entwines her fingers in mine. "My wife and I, we believe you may be able to manipulate a great age of music from a...."

I pause. Is it time to reveal this yet? Persephone shakes her head, no, it is not.

"From a what?" Eurydice says. Her voice is curious but also? Impatient.

"You were correct, Eurydice, Orpheus is coming for you," Persephone says. "He means to come collect you here. And we have a task for you, but you must learn some things from us first."

The drip, drip, drop from the River Styx sounds like the beginning of an uninspired modern composition that Eurydice can only stand to, listening awkwardly. She stands both stunned by the information and struck by the follow-through. As most mortals (and ghosts) do when they lack full comprehension of the situation, she repeats the last thing she heard back to us.

"Learn some things from you first," Eurydice says.

"Yes," we both say in dissonant melody.

"What do you mean to teach me?"

I stand, crossing the distance between Eurydice and myself, lowering my height to mortal height so as not to overwhelm her. When reaching for her face, I pause, considering first. There is a better way.

"May I touch your face?" I ask.

"Yes, Hades," she says.

I take Eurydice's chin in my hands and lift her eyes the slight distance up to mine. When she looks into them, she can see the truth of the dead, that I have no time for lies, tricks, or foolishness. That I have had eternity to play with, and I have since grown tired of games.

"Eurydice," I say (and I say something you know vaguely of already). "Eurydice, how would you like to become a muse?"

EURYDICE:

MEMORIES

So Andi and me went back to my dorm room that night. My room that'd been left empty for weeks since Orpheus had proposed. Since I put on the ring and abandoned this room, its laundry, and my independence. Like a loser.

I opened that familiar old door and threw my keys and my engagement ring at the closet. The ring made a dent more permanent than anything I'd ever promised Orpheus. Anything at all. He'd make a wife out of me one day?

No, not today.

Not even ever.

This room even *smelled* abandoned, the remnants of thrice-worn socks and the stalest of stale cigarettes. The saddest memory to come back to (and clean up). In a desperate effort to keep things normal, Andi went for the (actually) made bed. The only tidy thing in the room.

One of the last things I'd done before that ill-fated recital was changing the sheets, so at least those were clean. An attempt at a cleansing to get rid of any stain Orpheus left behind. Although pieces of him were scattered around the room. An ashtray filled with cigarette butts here, post-its saying everything from "BRB" to "ILU" dangling there, his old Bad Brains t-shirt on slung over the back of my computer chair, still.

I was always shit at throwing things out. Especially men.

I was such shit at throwing Orpheus out that the only impact I'd made was left on the closet door, echoed by the fact that Orpheus was the reason we were hiding in this room. This room was a tomb to my indecision. Andi was pretending they were unmoved, but I could tell by the fact that they weren't moving that they really were upset.

"So we stay here, right?" they said. "With your mysterious plan."

I flopped on the end of the bed, legs dangling off, backpack propping me up at an uncomfortable angle. "I have to tell you something,"

"What?" Andi smirked, but the shaking edges of their mouth betrayed their worry.

"I think," I said. "No, I *know* that Aristaeus wants to kill you."

Andi narrowed their eyes and sat up, crossing their legs, laying their long and spindly arms across their calves. "Wants to what me?"

"Kill you."

"Eurydice, this is college. Not a show on the CW."

I sat up, too, because Andi and I were so psychically linked that we couldn't help mirroring one another. So, I sat up, crossing my own legs, and took their hands in mine, running my thumbs over their palms. Finally, the sigh that broke against a held sob caught Andi's attention.

"Hey," they said, pulling a hand away to wipe tears from my face. "Hey, you and me. We're gonna be all right?"

"Yeah?" I asked.

"Yeah."

Except it turned out not to be true.

Andi and I lasted two days of skipping classes and doing a bunch of laundry and vacuuming before we thought that Hector had turned us in. My initial reaction? *The little shit. Awkward as fuck asshole couldn't keep five feet from the Dean on a good day, but when faced with juicy dirt, of course, his orbit shrunk.*

At least that's what we thought.

But the reality was much, much worse.

Andi got an email from the Dean of Students on the third morning, asking them to come in and bring "your girlfriend, Eurydice, as this concerns her as well." So we arrived, because we had to. Cause being expelled wasn't an option.

We arrived after smoking a bunch of

cigarettes and drinking the last of my way-stale coffee that was (at one time) really good but after three months of sitting as bagged grounds in my room was barely palatable. So basically, we both arrived in no mood to see the Dean. And in no mood to see the others there: Orpheus, Aristaeus, and Hector.

The Dean was a woman who looked like she wanted to be Grace Jones but was born with a David Bowie fashion sense. She did have Grace Jones's hair, which I super respected. Her clothes were similarly from the two musicians' heyday: red blazer with shoulder pads for days, a purple sweater so loud that it almost hurt to look at her. The office was furnished similarly 80's style.

Unlike Aristaeus, I could respect a commitment this long to an aesthetic.

Orpheus, of course, looked relieved to see me. Relieved in that way that I knew was fake. His eyes were up to something the same way they were that day at the recital. That *gotcha* sort of way. But his body language did all the right things: hands over heart, big sigh, aborted attempt to stand.

Hector, however, looked like a shit-ton of sixteenth notes that had been suddenly thrown into the wrong composition and, much like sixteenth notes, just wanted to quickly get the fuck on with it and out of here.

Aristaeus just took up space. Like usual. What an asshole.

The Dean folded her hands and looked up at Andi and me.

"Andromeda, Eurydice, come join us."

Andi grimaced and moved to sit as far away from the three dudes, leaving me sitting next to my unbeknownst-to-him-*ex*-fiancé who reached out and grabbed my hand. Gross. I let him hold it for a hot second before retreating into the sleeve of my clean and fabric-softened favorite black sweatshirt. (It said: *I Love You To Death* on it.)

(In retrospect, poor choice of clothing for the day.)

The Dean folded her fingers together in front of her and began speaking in the a tone of voice that was both monotone and repetitive. As if she was trying to believe the story herself. The way that a person tries to make sense of something unbelievable.

And what she said was:

"Andromeda, Eurydice, you are here because Orpheus and Aristaeus went looking for Eurydice and found Hector with Andromeda's things. Hector here said that he was forced not to tell anyone where you two girls were, and eventually when Orpheus began to cry—"

I spoke up, uncharacteristic of me, but this was a farce as transparent as Mozart's *Village Musicians.*

"Hold on. Excuse me for a moment Dean."

"Of course."

"Okay. Orpheus went looking for me and instead found *Hector* with *Andi's* things on him? That doesn't strike you as weird?"

The Dean shook her head; her jacket did not move. Really, really 80s.

"If I can say: Andi and I were in my room this whole time because Orpheus's boyfriend had threatened us. Aristaeus, who is standing right there." Aristaeus didn't even blink like a rattlesnake doesn't when it's watching you before striking. "Why didn't Orpheus, my fiancé, come looking for me in my room, where I'd probably be if I wasn't in his room or Andi's room? I mean, Orpheus is a pretty smart guy. Why did he go looking for Hector?"

The Dean's eyes got comically wide, betraying about ten years of Botox. Either that or she totally wasn't surprised by this surprise. Either way, the Dean was all we had right now, and we had to put out faith in her. All bets were on the table.

She turned her attention to Orpheus, Aristaeus, and Hector. "Well, boys, do you care to amend your story?"

Hector fidgeted so hard that his keys jingled in his pocket, and his backpack fell to his elbows. A master manipulator, he was not. He revealed himself at that time to be exactly what he was because he spoke up.

"Andi and Eurydice came to me. They seemed like they were scared of Orpheus and

Aristaeus, Miss Dean. The problem is." He paused, shuffling his sneakers so hard on the carpet he was gonna make sparks. "The problem is that I wanted to protect them, Andi. And I guess Eurydice by proxy. So when Orpheus came to me, I. I had to protect them. Andi. And I guess Eurydice. But Orpheus got *mad*. Mad mad."

The Dean nodded in the way that mothers nod when their kids are finally getting to the truth of how the cookie jar shattered on the ground.

"And then Aristaeus started throwing things and, and, and. I came here. I didn't know what to do."

"You aren't the one in trouble, Hector," the Dean said.

Her voice was soft as the cashmere of her sweater. I swore I could almost believe it. From the way Hector nearly melted to the ground, it was obvious that he actually did.

"So I can go?"

"You may go."

Hector left in a blur of gangly legs and thrice-slamming door. He hadn't looked at us once and honestly looked like he hadn't slept in days. The worry we'd caused him probably kept him up the whole time Andi and I had been cleaning and laundry-ing and fucking. I owed him big time. Big, big time.

Orpheus, however, sighed. But it was more of a hiss.

"Aristaeus has a flair for the dramatic," he said, leaning back, confident in his bullshit artistry. "I am sure this can all be explained."

"Oh, please explain it." The Dean grinned at him, turning her full attention to him now that the room had cleared out a little. She looked him over, assessing Orpheus not as the brilliant musician but as the brilliant asshole. When she spoke again, she was still looking at Orpheus. "Andromeda, Eurydice? You may go. I have more questions for Orpheus and Aristaeus here."

Orpheus leaned in. "I can explain."

The Dean leaned in as well. "I'd love that."

Orpheus leaned back and ran a shaking hand through his unwashed hair while he looked at me, his lip also curling. Andi's fingers gripped their chair as they rose and as the tension in the room tightened from D to E string.

I didn't want to leave, but I stood up slowly and walked to the door as Aristaeus opened his mouth and took a breath. The door shut behind us on his long and drawn-out, "Well, *actually*."

That was the middle of the end.

THE AFTERLIFE:
PRESENT DAY

Persephone had brought up a potential hitch to our "Eurydice: The Muse" plan sometime back when we were feeding Cerberus. While the not-so-evil hound of the Afterlife devoured his evening meal in three ceramic dog bowls, Persephone leaned across the counter and took my hands in hers.

"She was already a muse to Orpheus. You know that, dear."

"I do, yes."

Persephone is, was, and always will be right about most things earthly and material. There is a sense of knowledge that I lack being down here, eternally, only grasping pieces of life as a highlight reel from the Fates, the Instructors, and the conversations the ghosts have witnessed via my godsight.

But Persephone, the true life of me, knows what I do not.

"What if the offer is too small?" she says.

She said and licked her lips in a way that was such a mortal gesture that it made me think of what it would be to be alive, to be mortal. To understand what it is that the living seeks in one another, this connection, these small things. Small things are what makes a man, a woman, a person, a god fall in love. The way Persephone licks her lips and her hair always falls from behind her ear moments after she tucks it away are the things that make me empty when she spirits away for the spring.

When she returns, they are the things that make me whole again.

Now, as I hold Eurydice's chin in my hand, as her spirit-self trembles with my whole dark divinity this close to her. I could shatter her to pieces if I wanted to: prevent her from going Beyond, lock her forever in this place, send her to paradise or earthly purgatory for reincarnation to live out her misdeeds again and again.

With Persephone behind me, my anger, my fury is sated. I will not, I would not. She tempers my fury, my rage. She fits in neatly the other half of my heart, the one that reminds me what it is to be compassionate, to be kind. To offer solace rather than solitude.

Eurydice continues to tremble as I wait patiently. Persephone rises and walks over, moves my hand away, and leads me back to our shared throne. She knows what we must do, what we both must do.

"Eurydice," Persephone says. "Will you be a muse? For us?" She pauses, tucking her hair behind her ear. "Will you be a muse to those struggling as you once did to rid themselves of a burdensome lover they cannot shake? To teach them that they are worthy? That their music is worthy?" She lays her hand on my bare knee, her smile calming Eurydice's tremors. "Will you do that? For yourself? For others?"

There is a drip, drip, drop of the River Styx. A moan from Cerberus as he rolls over. A sigh rattles through Eurydice, and then.

"Yes," she says. "Yes, I would."

"Good," Persephone says. "Let's get started then."

All three of us rise (the two of us and Cerberus) and lead Eurydice through The Hall room and into our living quarters. These are, as I can see with my godsight, both shocking and comforting to Eurydice. They look as a modern kitchen would, familiar yet out of place to her.

Faux stone countertops, a four-burner stove, dishwasher, and a small refrigerator tucked into an out-of-the-way alcove, stone steps leading up to a door out to a yard with olive trees and plenty of room for the 'dog.'

Eurydice halts at the door.

"You did not expect this?" I ask.

Nothing from her.

"We are modern gods," I say.

"Modern gods," Eurydice says.

"Yes," says Persephone. "Hades is very particular to the stove."

"Of course he is," Eurydice says as if this all makes sense.

I can see that it does not.

When Eurydice walks in, she touches the stove and dishwasher and oven to see if they're real. They are (metaphysically). "Aren't you gods? Can't you magic up food? Don't you not have to eat?"

Persephone shrugs and unwraps a slice of cheese direct from Wisconsin. "Yes, but cooking is fun. Cleaning is fun. Eating is fun."

Eurydice makes a face at *Cleaning is fun* but sits down when I pull out a chair for her at the counter. She folds her hands like I do, likely as she has no idea what else to do with them. Persephone eats another slice of wrapped cheese.

"So, to become a muse, you must apply two of the teachings you learned in your time here in the Afterlife: Hauntings and Threads of Fate," I say.

I am still in my cowl and hip shroud. Chest bare, hair lanky. Persephone is still in her seafoam diaphanous dress. This is not our normal house clothing, but the kitchen itself seemed too much already.

"But I was terrible at both those classes," Eurydice says.

"Not so," Persephone says. "You were just terrible enough."

"Terrible enough," Eurydice repeats.

She has a habit of doing this. Perfect for a muse.

"Yes," I say. "You were not good at not being seen, which is what a muse needs, and you were not good at cutting off someone's thread simply due to the facts presented. You wanted to consider the cause and effect, the environment, the others involved."

"Exactly," Persephone says, ironing out her cheese wrapper with her hands. "Muses are beings who live in right and wrong. They live in the arts."

Eurydice folds and refolds her hands three times, then four.

"When do I begin?" she asks.

"You already have," Persephone says. "Your true beginning will be your first trial."

"Which is?" Eurydice asks.

I look at Persephone, who looks at me. She nods and stands to get out pomegranate juice from the refrigerator and some glasses. Ice clinks against the glass as I turn and reach toward Eurydice, and, of course, her hands retreat from mine (as I expected).

"Orpheus."

"What about him?" she asks. Her hands against her chest. Wringing once again.

"He's coming here tomorrow to fetch you. To bring you back to him."

"What do... what do I do about that?" Eurydice asks as Persephone sets a glass of pomegranate juice in front of her. She takes it, sips it, and considers for a moment. "What do you want me to do?"

"Do what you have to," I say. "Do what needs to be done."

EURYDICE:

MEMORIES

Orpheus and Aristaeus got a three-week suspension from social activities and classes. They were not allowed to use the music rooms, they were not allowed to come near either Andi or me. This meant that Orpheus could not perform his recital, or any of his gigs, and that any epic breakup I had planned with him would have to wait almost a month.

Andi and I were standing in front of the diner near the Dean's office, smoking cigarettes and waiting for a table, when Orpheus and Aristaeus walked up. We'd only heard about their punishment from Hector, who'd heard it from someone who'd heard it from someone.

Gossip spreads super-fast. Faster than thirty feet.

It had been ninety minutes, and Orpheus and Aristaeus couldn't hold off breaking their restraining order for even that long. "Shit happens," he even said when he walked right the fuck up to me. "And then you die."

I frowned at both of them. Andi gave me a long *why the fuck are we still standing here* glance. Fifteen minutes was a long wait for a table at the diner, so I nodded my head down toward the cafeteria, and Andi turned in that direction, catching the hint. But, as I moved to follow, Orpheus grabbed my hand.

"Where's your ring?" he asked.

"What ring?"

I was always horrible at bullshittery.

Andi froze. Time froze. Birds kept singing 'cause they're fucking birds, and people rode by on bicycles screaming things at each other cause who cares about anyone else overhearing gossip, right? But for us four, it was a standoff worthy of the *William Tell Overture.* Just as ridiculous and bombastic and likely to end in just as much fanfare.

"Your engagement ring," Orpheus said, a sneer on his face. "The one I gave you 'cause we're getting married, Eurydice? Or do you not want to marry me anymore? Is that something you were keeping from me too? Along with your musical farces of my work and your destruction of my reputation with the school Administration?"

Andi licked their lips, their hands balling into fists as they ground their cigarette out under their boot heel. They were ready to fight, but Andi was short, skinny, with long hair and a chunky cardigan. And I was a music major who had to protect her hands, one of which was being held by one of our enemies.

The other one I'd neglected to tell Andi was 90% asshole and 10% spite.

I took a deep breath, looking Orpheus right in the eyes. I placed my other hand on his arm and held it tight to keep it from shaking. Setting my jaw for a second, I steeled everything as strong as upright bass strings and said.

"No, Orpheus, of course, I still want to marry you."

What a liar.

And Orpheus knew it. He narrowed his eyes at me, gripping my hand harder.

"So, where's the ring?"

"I take it off to shower, probably didn't put it back on when Andi got the Dean's email."

"Shitty Dean," Aristaeus said, heavy on the Shitty.

My legs were shaking so hard that I was having trouble standing. Andi was muttering behind their clenched teeth, and Aristaeus was looking at their nails the way people do in books or songs but not real life. Orpheus, however, was looking at me.

"Come with me," he said.

And pulled me by the hand. I had no choice but to follow as Aristaeus fell in behind me, and then Andi behind him. These two men who were ordered not to stay near us had me hemmed in, one gripping my hand so hard that his nails bit my skin, the other? A shadow on my back.

Andi was struggling to keep up.

Orpheus and Aristaeus had a couple of things going for them. First, Academia moves very slowly. Second, because Academia moves very slowly, he still had access to his practice room. Third, it was really early in the morning, and no one was in the practice rooms yet. Fourth, and this was the worst one: Orpheus's practice room was sound-proof.

So when he led me, still pinching my hand, into his practice room and threw me in there, locking all four of us in, I was shocked. I thought the school would protect us (how foolish). I thought we'd be safer than that (how silly).

Nope.

Thing was, people saw us walking. And those people were talking as we traveled, pointing and yelling. "Someone do something! Someone has to do something!" But they all stood there gawking. Thing is, in these situations, people rarely do anything, but everyone says they're gonna do something.

Someone did do something, eventually. They'd arrive in five minutes. However, it would be three minutes too late. Thank you, Hector, who was the one who acted. Always the one to act. Hector, for all his faults, was really an amazing guy.

Hector, in retrospect, didn't have many faults.

So, all of this took two minutes. I was on the floor, sitting with my hands against the wall. Ready to jump up and run at the door that Orpheus and Andi were blocking. Orpheus held the key dangling from his middle finger, and Andi pointed three of their fingers at his sunken chest.

"You little shit," they said. "You thought you were in trouble before? You're gonna be expelled for this. I'm gonna run your name through the dirt."

"He'll get famous for that," Aristaeus said, in his way of sounding bored. Like this whole situation was boring. But he was holding one of Orpheus's vintage King Snake guitars in his hand the way a soldier in a fantasy show would hold an axe.

Orpheus sighed and backed up to the wall.

"I just want an explanation, I just wanna talk this through."

"The time for talking is over, you small-dicked, big-ego fuckwad," Andi said. "Let Eurydice and I go, and I might, I just might, not tell the Dean."

"Shitty Dean," Aristaeus said again. Once again, heavy on the Shitty.

Orpheus's entire body crescendoed at that.

"I'm tired of you, Andi. I'm tired of you not acting like an adult and ruining everything.

Trying to steal my wife from me, ruin me, trying to turn people against me. What the shit do you have against me anyway? What the fuck did I ever do to you?"

Andi sighed so hard it practically shook the dust off the amps. I wanted to help them, I needed to help them. So I tried to get up, but before clearing two inches off the floor, Aristaeus had his hand on my shoulder, pushing me down.

"Sit down," he said. "Adults are talking."

"This one isn't an adult," Orpheus said. "Andi is a child. A petulant child."

"Fuck you, Orpheus. Fuck you and your music and pretention and boytoy."

"I am not a toy," Aristaeus said. I tried to get up again, now was the time to mention that snake fucker here didn't fucking care about anyone but himself. But nope, snake fucker pushed me back down to the floor again. "I said, sit down, Eurydice."

Aristaeus had stringy-guy strength, which I didn't expect. I kept falling back, glued to the ground, stuck there, even when Andi said, "Let me out, Orpheus. I'm leaving. Come on, Eurydice, we're leaving."

I could only shake my head.

The look on their face broke my heart a thousand times. My ribcage pierced into it as their expression grew sad, lost. They knew they'd lost me. But they didn't know how badly yet. So as I bit both lips to keep from crying and dug my ragged nails into the carpet so hard that they snagged to keep me from calling their name as Orpheus unlocked the door, and I heard their shuffle stomp shuffle of their footsteps as they walked away, as all that happened, I lost what was left of my love for Orpheus.

I threw it away right then and there.

Aristaeus was standing about two feet from me, strangling the neck of that King Snake guitar, when Orpheus approached me. He leaned over me, his voice shuddering with impatience.

"I need to know something, Eurydice," he said.

"What."

It was all I could say.

"Do you want to marry me or not?"

I looked at Aristaeus, I looked back at Orpheus. These two were meant for each other, the way Andi and I were meant for each other. These two fit one another so neatly they were codas of one another, the way Andi and I were harmonies of one another. Orpheus and I would never fit, we argued, we fought, we fucked poorly.

We were dissonance.

I needed less dissonance in my life.

Turning my attention back to Orpheus, I said, "You know...."

And then I shrugged.

"Enough of this," Aristaeus said, raising the

guitar high to swing it. "You need me in your life, not a whining girl."

"I'm not a girl," I said, my attention on Orpheus. "I'm a woman not a girl. Tell him that, tell him I'm not a girl, Orpheus. Please."

But Orpheus wasn't paying attention to me, his hands were raised toward Aristaeus. He was saying, "No. No, don't. No please don't. No."

I felt a swift breeze and then a splitting pain against the side of my head. There was a brief feel of warm blood as it ran down my scalp and hair, down my neck, dripping onto my shoulder. Aristaeus killed me with that gods-damned King Snake guitar. I know that much. I also know that my last words were, "What the fuck?"

I'm super not proud of that.

THE AFTERLIFE:
PRESENT DAY

At three o'clock, standard Death Time, Eurydice must attend mandatory Threads of Fate sewing lessons. Or did must, had musted? These lessons are no longer, as you well know. Her classmates are unaware of this decree, but they are aware that Eurydice has not been attending lessons the past two days and has arrived at this particular lesson two minutes past three o'clock Standard Death Time.

Eurydice, however, is not here to cut ties with Fate. She is here to say goodbye to a friend.

Penelope is at the front of the class, talking about how Fate weaves its way through our lives: through decision and indecision, through those we meet and those we pass by. Those we pass by could be those we meet, should we make the time, in another lifetime or circumstance.

Her hair is done up in three braids that intertwined around her head and down her back.

The longest one swinging like a dark pendulum as she speaks. Her hands swing in opposite time with her gestures, keeping up with the fickleness of fate and the true idea of time. Her smile is kind and gentle, like death itself.

But not dying. We covered that.

"That's where Fate comes in," Penelope says, holding a golden thread aloft. "What is the decision or indecision? Where do paths turn or converge?" Lowering her hands, she smiles at the ghosts and spirits gathered, all rapt in her story, as they, too, want to move Beyond, as they know Penelope will, after this class. "In my life, I was a weaver. I used thread and time to hold off what I thought was the inevitable—the news of my husband's death."

She glances to the side where Eurydice is waiting.

"Sometimes, we have to say our goodbyes far sooner than we want. I should have said goodbye to him long before. Given up my weaving and taken up with another man. My husband did not die, but he should have on his journey. He came back a changed man."

Eurydice knows (as Penelope says to the class) that many men are changed after achieving what they want.

The class converges on Penelope to say their congratulations. Still, she eventually can break away and come speak to Eurydice, who has been waiting, the class's curious eyes turning toward the pair: this Eurydice who has been absent for two whole days (if days do indeed exist here), and her friend Penelope who will be absent forevermore.

"Missed you," Penelope says to Eurydice.

"No," Eurydice says to Penelope. "I'll miss you more."

"If that's even possible," Penelope says, "where we're both going."

"Where you're going, maybe," Eurydice says, smiling a ghost smile up at Penelope, who will always be taller and have more bearing than Eurydice, no matter what form she takes. "Where I'm going? You're gonna be unforgettable."

"You cad."

Penelope smiles widely at Eurydice, but her eyes are sad. This is it. This is the short moment before the final goodbye. Now, what do both women say? Both women have said goodbye too many times to too many people.

Of course, they botch it.

"I wanna stay but—"

"Same. I gotta go, too."

They each shuffle their feet in front of the other, daring their best friend to move first. Wonder of wonders, it is Penelope who moves first. Brushing past her friend Eurydice and walking out into the hall. Eurydice follows and watches her as her braid swings in perfect rhythm to her steps—she is walking toward a door of golden light.

She is going Beyond.

Penelope disappears behind the door, and Eurydice lingers for a moment, thinking of all the things she didn't say. She never told Penelope how much she cared about her or thanked her, really for her friendship. Or how much she helped. Or any of that. Any of that mushy stuff that Eurydice wasn't good at in life and sure wasn't good at in death. She hadn't told Penelope that she was going to see Orpheus, who could be right now, this very moment, walking past the empanada shop (which meant Eurydice was late).

So she needs to get going.

She's got other things to do.

The hallway is colder and less forgiving without Penelope beside her, but Eurydice walks it anyway. She walks toward the entrance of the Afterlife. Past the patisseries and empanada shops, past the moors and the bogs. She walks up the mountain steppes to the entrance to the Afterlife, the black stone cavern where the steps lead down from the River Styx into this realm.

The steps are slick, yet not crumbling, they trickle with the black water and have since eternity. Yet this has not worn them down. Neither have the eons and eons of ghost feet traversing them with their burdens and woes. However, standing at the top step, Eurydice now sees a man, an entire man, a live man waiting and flipping a single coin.

She knows this man's ego is large enough to test the limit of the stairs.

His hair is still unruly, and where a concert t-shirt had hung from his skeletal frame, he is instead dressed in a wrinkled button-down (did he dress up for a funeral?). His jeans are so brand new that they still have the store-creases in them but are tucked into those same old scuffed and mistreated boots.

We all know who this is, but he bears introduction: this is Orpheus, and he has come to collect what he feels he lost. But he did not lose her? Did he? No, he threw her away. And she, Eurydice, is expecting him at the bottom of the stairs, which he steps down in all his grandiosity. Except this is a charade, for Eurydice alone.

Eurydice places her wispy hands on her ghost hips.

"You came a long way, Orpheus," she says. "You sure you can get back?"

"I have a good sense of direction," he says. "Eurydice, you don't belong here." His voice has that pompous attitude of musicians who think they're bigger than they are. Bigger than Zeus, as one said. Except that one was okay, he went Beyond. "I've come to take you home."

"Oh yeah?" Eurydice says. "You've come to take me home. Amazing, how're you gonna manage that since you have fare for one there in your hand."

"Fare for what?"

Orpheus's voice is percussive with confusion.

"You've got one coin in your hand," Eurydice says, still wearing the smirk she shared with Penelope. "That's one passage on the River Styx. One trip. So how're you gonna get both you out and me out?"

"Small oversight," Orpheus says with that same overconfidence. "Easily fixed."

"Is it?"

"Yeah," he says. He pauses, allowing the faux gravity to sink in. "Totally. Trust me. I got this."

He's still walking down the stairs, swaggered step after swaggered step. Like he's been practicing this moment in his mom's house, rehearsing it like he should have been rehearsing his recital, except that's right, he got expelled, arrested, and then released. Whoops.

A little backstory on Orpheus, he was an accomplice in Eurydice's murder. Pleaded innocent, except was caught due to multiple (multitudes) witnesses and his sound equipment catching a recording of the conversation. Two years have passed on Earth since Eurydice's unfair death, and Orpheus was released on good behavior and better lawyers.

However, he is not welcome back at the school (and hasn't had much luck getting into any other schools). So perhaps he thinks bringing Eurydice back is his magnum opus, his masterpiece, his ResserRequiem. But his music career might take off; awful people love a musician with a dark and checkered past.

"Sure, you got this, you always got this. I forgot that about you," Eurydice says, with the cold attitude of the dead. But what she's watching is his boots coming closer and closer to the Afterlife floor. I watch her eyes follow Orpheus's body, his movements. I watch her fingers twitch, counting out the beats.

"Why are you here?" Orpheus asks, now four steps from the Afterlife, still flipping his coin-fare. "I thought like, you'd be too good for this place."

"Waiting for you, clearly," Eurydice says. Three steps. "I mean, this is a way-station. Right? We all gotta wait for something. So I guess I was waiting for you, cause I'm not waiting for anything else. "

Orpheus pauses at three steps. "Huh. Doesn't that get boring? Waiting around? Being dead?"

"Not really," Eurydice says. "It's the dying part that's bad. Knowing how I died, that was the shitty part."

Orpheus starts walking again. Two steps. "Yeah, well, that wasn't my fault. Not really."

"Oh yeah," Eurydice says as Orpheus takes his last two steps and ends up on Afterlife ground. There's nothing special about Afterlife ground, not really. But he's close to Eurydice, and this is exactly what she wanted, it's written all over the relief in her ghost-shoulders and relaxed fingers. "Totally not your fault, totally that Aristotle guy's."

"Aristaeus."

Orpheus walks closer to Eurydice, twirling the coin in his fingers. Only a few more steps now. Patience, Eurydice.

"Yeah, whatever. I forgot about him."

"You. You forgot about him? You forgot about the man I loved? The man that I owe my musical genius to? The man that saved me from prison? You forgot about the love of my life?"

Gotcha.

Literally, too, Orpheus is standing right in front of Eurydice as she reaches out and snatches that coin away from him. Snatches it away and puts it in her ghost pockets. Once deep enough for an entire life, it now holds Orpheus's fate in them. She shoves her own hands in and leans back on her ghost-heels.

"The love of your life. And I don't see you coming to *rescue him*."

Orpheus fumes, not yet realizing the coin is gone.

"He's in prison, and it's your fault," he says.

Silly, silly man. What's that they say about fools rushing in? Well, this man has done it, and let's just say he's made a very large miscalculation.

Eurydice walks past Orpheus and on up the stairs on her way out of the Afterlife.

"This was a good talk, Orpheus, glad to see you haven't changed." She smiles. "It's a relief, really. A super relief. The registration is just past the gift shop, across from the Bean There, Done That coffee place."

"Regi-what?"

He pats himself down for the coin, searches the ground for it, and lifts his boots. But no, it's gone. I know that, Eurydice knows that, now Orpheus knows that as Eurydice climbs the stairs out and up toward the River Styx, leaving Orpheus turning incorporeal, his hand outstretched.

Way to lose your head, buddy.

EPILOGUE THE FIRST:
in which eurydice muses on present-day earth

Of course, the first person I pick to muse is Andi.

A muse doesn't get assigned to someone I learned as much learning as there was to do about musing. It's that we get called to someone, sort of like being prayed to, and then we sort of show up and inspire them. And Andi had been calling out to me so much while I was gone.

They missed me, which broke my heart. I guess I missed them too, if I had the capacity to miss anyone in the Afterlife? I don't know if I did. Ghosts only feel two things: fear and uncertainty. At least, me as a ghost.

Until the musing lessons started.

Anyway, that's a lot of boring stuff about How To Be Inspiring and How To Stand Around Being Sort Of Not Invisible and How To Accidentally Inspire Greatness which apparently I was brilliant at even when I was trying not to be, so I guess muse.

But also, anyway, Andi.

They missed me so much that they decided to start taking piano lessons, and I sat next to them in their piano practice sessions in my old practice room and gently lay my hand on theirs. And I swear to fuck, they'd sigh, and their playing would loosen, and their body would loosen.

And you know what? They got good.

I slept in the chair in their room but gave them some privacy when they had Hector or their girlfriend over or for other stuff. I'm not a creepy creeper, never have been. I also wandered the college campus now that I wasn't seeing it at Orpheus's heels, and it wasn't so bad, actually.

It was a beautiful place, full of towering evergreen trees and mountain paths and singing, so much singing. Graduation is this year: the year Orpheus, Andi, and I were all supposed to walk the stage and get our useless Bachelor's degrees. Andi was the only one up there. They said my name at the ceremony and Andi cried a little. That afternoon, Andi took their guitar and their long-time girlfriend out for a picnic in the woods. When Andi brought the guitar out and said, "I wrote a song for you." The girlfriend said, "Seriously?" And Andi said, "No, I swear this is not bad."

It really wasn't cause we worked on it together.

When the girlfriend leaned over and kissed Andi when they were done, I looked away but remembered the taste of their mouth: ashes and honey lip balm.

I had to go back to Persephone for more lessons. Muses start as ghostly things but can become corporeal, shapeshifting humans. After musing Andi as an incorporeal form ('cause they really had been praying for me so hard), I'm meant to go back to Persephone to learn to take corporeal form.

Which'll be pretty cool. Cause right now, at this very moment, I'm watching Andi put away their guitar, pull a box out of their pocket, and open it for their girlfriend, whose hands are over her mouth.

She says, "Yes."

Is it too soon? I've been dead for two years. Andi should move on.

And I should too.

EPILOGUE THE SECOND:
In which hades gets on
with the rest of eternity

That was the tale of Eurydice and Orpheus. Well, more than a tale, really. An overture of young love gone wrong. No, a symphony of missteps and wrong notes; of fate (no gods) playing their hands. It ended well, though. Don't you think? I like to think. Persephone likes to think so too, she told me before she left for another of her Earthly sabbaticals.

She promised me more hot dogs this time.

What can I say? The woman has good taste, both in mortals and food.

Cerberus and I remain in the Afterlife as it continues in its own ephemeral way. Marked by bells that mean nothing except for the humans that give them meaning. They call it magical thinking on Earth, so here? Here we put a bell on it. I send souls Beyond; send souls back to Earth for another go at getting it right. And occasionally (very occasionally), a soul got eternal punishment.

Can't tell you who, though.

Cause that's cheating.

Can tell you that the Fates are very pleased with Persephone, and Eurydice continues to impress upon burgeoning musicians the importance of art and falling in love for the sake of falling in love. As she once said, bad romance was something Lady Gaga got right. It does do a musician well. I have to agree, it does make for delicious art.

My godsight, however, is limited only to the Afterlife. So I concentrate on empanada houses, on this one woman drinking her cardamom tea. She is drinking alone and watching the cloud cover yet another grey sky on yet another grey day. For a ghost, she surely does consider quite a lot about quite a lot of things.

I lean forward on the kitchen counter and concentrate further. Because there will always be other souls like Eurydice, like Penelope. There have been thousands before and will be thousands since. Perhaps this next one is her.

Perhaps this next one is Hope.